Get Along,
Little Dogies

The

Lone ★ Star

Journals

Book 1

Get Along,
Little Dogies

The Chisholm Trail Diary of
Hallie Lou Wells

South Texas, 1878

Lisa Waller Rogers

This book was set in Galliard, and Cosmic Two. The paper used in this book meets the minimum requirements of ANSI/NISO Z39.48-1992 (R1997). ∞

Although her diary is based on historical events, Hallie Lou Wells is a fictional character.

Series design by Joan Osth; book design by Bryce Burton; cover art by Mary Ann Jacob

Library of Congress Cataloging-in-Publication Data
    Rogers, Lisa Waller, 1955-
    Get along, little dogies : the Chisholm Trail diary of Hallie Lou Wells : south Texas, 1878 / by Lisa Waller Rogers.
        p. cm. — (The Lone Star journals ; bk. 1)
    Summary: Fictional diaries of a fourteen-year-old girl accompanying a cattle drive along the Chisolm Trail in 1878.
    ISBN 0-89672-446-8 (cloth) — ISBN 0-89672-448-4 (paper)
    1. Chisholm Trail—Juvenile fiction. [1. Chisholm Trail—Fiction.
2. Cattle drives—Fiction. 3. Cowboys—Fiction. 4. West (U.S.)—Fiction.
5. Diaries—Fiction.] I. Title.
    PZ7.R62568 Ge 2001
    [Fic]—dc21

                                    00-011879

01 02 03 04 05 06 07 08 09 / 9 8 7 6 5 4 3 2 1

Texas Tech University Press
Box 41037
Lubbock, Texas 79409-1037 USA

800-832-4042
ttup@ttu.edu
www.ttup.ttu.edu

To John Andrew and Carolyn King Waller,
my loving parents
always faithfully at my side

Fame is like a vapor
Popularity an accident
Riches take wings
Those who cheer today
Curse tomorrow
One thing only endures
Character

Tombstone inscription
Grave of Texas Governor Robert Allan Shivers
(1907–1985)
Texas State Cemetery
Austin, Texas

Get Along, Little Dogies

The Chisholm Trail Diary of Hallie Lou Wells

South Texas, 1878

Hallie Lou's World

Family

Hallie Lou—a spirited, capable teenage girl
   growing up in the South Texas brush
   country

Papa—Hallie Lou's father, J. R. Wells, who
   owns a South Texas ranch, the Rockin' W

Mama—Hallie Lou's mother, who takes care of
   everyone on her ranch lovingly

Ray—Hallie Lou's brother, who is all boy and
   almost man

Gussie—Hallie Lou's sweet and funny little sister, who is six years old

2

Ranch Hands and Servants

Dovey Mae—Hallie Lou's lady servant and best friend

Gabby—the house cook at the Rockin' W and Dovey Mae's mother

Mister Ab—the ranch foreman and trail boss

Jeb Chapman—the "straw boss," second in command to trail boss

Cookie—the cook for the cowboys

Joe One-Wing—Cookie's assistant

Chico—the horse wrangler

The Rowdy King Boys—three brothers from Seguin, Henry, John R., and Will, who are trail hands on the cattle drive

Little Rusty—a trail hand

Bud—a trail hand

Ed—a trail hand

Butch Craven—a trail hand

The Animals

El Tuerto—the one-eyed bell steer who leads the herd to Dodge

Ole Red—the feisty "outlaw" bull

Mrs. Bubbies—the bell cow who pulls up the rear on the cattle drive to watch over the slow little dogies

China Doll—a skittish Siamese cat

Rosie—Hallie Lou's strawberry roan pony

Dooley—Jeb Chapman's dog

Victoria, Texas

1878

Sunday, April 7, 1878

I behaved horribly today! I don't know what came over me. All Dovey Mae did was to ask me a simple question.

"Miss Hallie," she asked, "which do you want to wear to the dance—your peach organdy or your blue silk?" She laid the dresses side by side on my canopy bed.

I sat at my vanity. I had my back to her. I did not turn around. I crossed my arms over my chest and pushed out my lower lip.

"What does it matter which dress I wear?" I snapped. "Everybody who will be at the dance has already seen them both ninety-nine times!"

The minute I said it I wanted to take it back. I turned to apologize, but Dovey had slipped out of the room.

I don't know why I got mad about the dance. I'm actually looking forward to that dance. It's just that remembering the dance reminded me of the roundup. And remembering the roundup reminded me of the cattle drive. And remembering both the roundup and the cattle drive reminded me of something that's really been troubling me lately.

Boys! That's what's been troubling me. Boys! They get to do all the fun stuff—like the roundup, which starts in eight days! Then, to make matters worse, they get to drive those rounded-up cattle to Dodge City, Kansas. Guess who gets left back at the ranch? The girls!

Life is so unfair to girls! We need adventure, too. I can ride and rope and brand as well as any boy. Why, even when I was too young for horses, I rode tree limbs! Dovie and I used to gallop about on our stick horses and rope anything that moved. China Doll, our Siamese cat, still runs when she sees me coming!

I'd die to go to a fancy city like Dodge. . . .

Monday, April 8, 1878

Dovey Mae didn't come to my room tonight. She always comes in at bedtime to do my hair. I love it when she takes out my hairpins and lets my hair fall loose around my shoulders. Then, very slowly, she brushes my hair. She never yanks my scalp even if she does come across a nasty tangle. The brush glides through my long, reddish-brown, wavy hair.

Dovey likes the waves and the red. She says, "I wish I had your hair, Miss Hallie." Her hair is as straight as a board and as black as night. I think it is lovely.

In the daytime, she shampoos my hair. For special occasions, she rinses it in soft rainwater she collects in a wooden barrel out back. For two months, Dovey's been saving up rainwater for the big dance on the 27th.

I just had a terrible thought! What if she's so boiling mad at me that she throws out that rainwater!

While Dovey brushes, she sings incredibly beautiful Spanish songs. I get drowsy. When she has brushed my hair one hundred strokes (I do the counting), she lays the brush aside. With fast fingers, she braids my thick hair. Then she pats me on the shoulders and says, "*¡Hecho!*" (Done!)

We hug. Holding an oil lamp, she cuts across the courtyard to get to her house. From the parlor, Mama sees the flicker of Dovey's lamp. Mama then lays aside her needlework and rises. Papa is so used to this routine that he does not even look up from his paper. Mama can see Dovey leaving because our ranch house is shaped like a horseshoe. Every room has giant windows facing the center courtyard.

Mama always comes to put Gussie, my six-year-old sister, and me to bed. Ray, my nineteen-year-old brother, puts himself to bed. He says he's too old to be tucked in. No matter how old I get, I still want Mama to tuck me in. Especially tonight.

Tuesday, April 9, 1878

I woke up before the sun today. I tried to go back to sleep but I just lay in my bed and felt bad about the way I'd treated Dovey. She's still avoiding me.

I tiptoed barefoot over to my desk and lit my lamp. (Gussie could sleep through an earthquake!) I threw open the windows. In came the most magnificent breeze! It flutters the curtains and carries the sweet smell of chinaberry blossoms. The morning air feels good on my skin. Now I feel clean and fresh and poetic. I will write, I thought. Writing clears my head.

I'd give anything to take back the mean words I said to Dovey. She and I are practically sisters, even though she is my maid. Her real name is "Paloma Maria," which means "Dove Mary" in Spanish. When we were six, I nicknamed her "Dovey Mae." It's a perfect name for her, too. She is as gentle as a dove. (And I, Hallie Lou Wells, am as mean as a snake!)

Dovey is already fifteen. I'll be fifteen in July. Dovey was born here on the ranch. Papa brought her people here from Mexico.

Before the War Between the States, my papa, J. R. Wells, went on a cattle-buying trip to Mexico. His journey took him through a poor village. The people there were nothing but skin and bones. They begged Papa to buy their skinny cattle. He looked around. The corn in their fields hung withered on the stalks. Their creek was as dry as dust. Without food and water, how were these people to survive?

Papa made the villagers an offer. "Come and live on my ranch, the Rockin' W," he said, in Spanish. "I'll pay you good wages and build you houses that keep out the rain and the cold. When you are sick, Mrs. Wells will give you medicine. You have my word that, on the Rockin' W, you will never know another day of want."

The entire village loaded up their oxcarts and followed Papa to our ranch on Coleto Creek. That was twenty years ago. These Mexican families are still here, serving us. And, because Papa has kept his word, he is their hero.

The sun must be coming up because I just heard the peacock cry. I see him now. He's strutting around the courtyard fanning his feathers. Above him in the chinaberry tree perches the peahen, his "wife," as Gussie calls her. Last summer, Papa bought both birds for Mama when he was on a trip to . . .

Hey! A trip . . . That gives me a great idea! I know exactly how to make it up to Dovey—

Wednesday, April 10, 1878

Roundup starts Monday! A lovely, cool rain is falling—

Thursday, April 11, 1878

It's close to midnight—way too late for me to be awake. Mama put Gussie to bed hours ago! But I just cannot shut my eyes. Excitement is spilling out all over me.

The roundup—it's starting! Our ranch is the headquarters for this spring's grand cattle hunt. All day long, South Texas ranchers and their cowboys have been arriving here. They're still awake, too. Since dinner, they've been milling around out in the courtyard.

They're laughing and talking. I love the smell of their cigarette smoke drifting in my window.

By the light of the moon, I see their silhouettes. The ends of their cigarettes glow round and red. As they talk, the red dots bob up and down in their mouths. One man takes the cigarette out of his mouth and makes a gesture with it. It leaves a streak of fire in the air like a comet with a long tail. He's telling a story.

He's probably telling how he almost got Ole Red. Ole Red is a big, scrappy, long-legged, Longhorn bull that has been hiding in the brush for over seven years. No cowboy can work him out in the open or dab a rope on him. Plenty, though, have tried. Especially Mister Ab, our ranch foreman! He can tell more stories about Ole Red than anyone. When Mister Ab talks about Ole Red, he lowers his voice to a hush. You'd think he was talking about a ghost, he acts so spooked.

The gathering is breaking up. The ranchers are moseying over to our guesthouse. Their cowboys will sleep in our bunkhouse. I guess it's time for me, too, to hit the hay. . . .

Friday, April 12, 1878

I made my tutor mad today. Lately, I'm getting mighty good at upsetting people.

I was out of sorts even before we started our lessons. Everyone on the ranch was getting ready for the roundup but Gussie and me! It wasn't fair! We girls were chained to our books while the boys zipped freely about.

From our schoolhouse, we could see cowboys filling water barrels, chopping wood, and loading the supply wagon with pots, pans, food, bedrolls, and branding irons. Some were squatting by the fire, dipping rags in skillets of bacon grease and rubbing it onto their saddles, boots, and harnesses. Others were over by the washhouse, mending holes in their saddle blankets, washing them, and hanging them in the sun to dry.

I watched as Cookie, the cowboy cook, bent over a kettle of beans. He raised a spoonful to his lips.

What would it be like, I wondered, to go with them on the roundup? . . .

Just then my tutor, Miss Strickland, screeched, "Harriet Lucretia! Recite Shakespeare's 18th Sonnet—on the double!" My daydream bubble burst.

I jumped. "Oh!" I said, rising quickly. I cleared my throat and began:

> Shall I compare thee to a summer's day?
> Thou art more lovely and more temperate.
> Rough winds do shake . . .

I only got that far because, just then, somebody yelled across the yard, "HEY, COOKIE!" It was only natural that I stopped reciting to see who was yelling so.

It was Joe One-Wing. He's Cookie's helper. He and Chico were leaning against the chinaberry tree braiding ropes.

Once he had Cookie's attention, Joe continued. "If you want them wheel rims for your chuck wagon, you'd better hightail it over to Smitty's! By sundown, he'll be knee-deep in mustangs!"

Smitty puts shoes on the wild mustangs after Chico breaks them. At roundup and on the cattle drive, cowboys need seven horses apiece. Cow work is hard. Horses get tired. Chico's good about seeing that the working cowboys always have a fresh mount.

I regained my poise. "Uh . . . where was I?" I muttered sheepishly, returning from yet another daydream.

"Young lady," said Miss Strickland, in her starchiest voice, "your behavior is atrocious! Sit down this instant and memorize page 112 of the *Webster's School Dictionary!*"

Then in strolled my papa.

"That will be all for today," he announced, dismissing Miss Strickland with a brisk wave of his hand.

"Yippee!" we cried. Giggling and jumping up and down, Gussie and I smothered Papa in kisses and flew out the door.

Good old Papa. He always saves the day. But how will he explain this early dismissal to Mama? She's very strict about our schooling. She wants Gussie and me to become "proper young ladies." We must sew, bake, sing, play piano, quote Scripture, speak French, do sums, and write a pretty hand.

Papa agrees with this kind of learning—to a point. He wants us to learn to be ranchers as well. "Along with Ray," he is fond of reminding Mama, "our girls will one day run the ranch."

Miss Strickland's probably sore at me. But Dovey Mae's not. I told her about our trip. Now, I'll have to watch for just the right moment to ask Papa about it.

Saturday, April 13, 1878

Bandits are on the loose! The sheriff rode out here in the rain to tell us. Last night, he said, they attacked the Marshall Ranch near Skidmore. The robbers tied up the family, ransacked the house, and stole twenty horses. Other ranchers have reported cattle missing.

All through this dark and stormy night, an armed guard will keep watch outside my door. It blazes like daylight outside. Papa directed the men to stake torches from the hen house to the smokehouse and beyond. Even so, with the rain coming down in sheets and the wind blowing so hard, it's next to impossible to see anything, much less keep a good lookout for bandits who might murder us in our beds.

Up in the watchtower, Papa, Ray, and all our sharpest cowboys will share the night shift. Before this night is over, Cookie's legs will ache. He'll climb up and down that ladder with pots and pots of strong coffee for the lookout boys. Mister Ab is getting up in years, so he will oversee ground operations. His legs are a little creaky these days.

My heart is beating like a drum. I just know I'll never get any sleep.

Mama says this is when to call on the Almighty. He will calm my troubled soul. I will pull the covers over my head and say the Lord's Prayer again and again until blessed sleep finally overtakes me.

> Our Father, who art in heaven,
>   Hallowed be Thy Name . . . .

Sunday, April 14, 1878

Afternoon

Today is Palm Sunday. Even though Ray and Papa were on watch most the night, they still went with us into Victoria for church. Six guards on horseback rode alongside our buggy. They were armed to the teeth with six-shooters and Winchester rifles.

In silence we sloshed (it's still raining!) along that old familiar road. Never has that drive seemed so long. All five of us were tense, eagle-eyed, looking around every bend and peeking behind every cactus for bandits. Once we heard a weird grunt off the side of the road. We were sure our lives were over! It turned out to be nothing but a mean mama javelina with her piglets.

She wanted to cross the road and our buggy had gotten in her way. Mama laughed first, then Papa, and then the three of us young ones in the back. Laughing did us a world of good.

I thought we would never get to town. My red flannel petticoat scratched my legs. Mosquitoes bit my neck. But I did not dare to complain. What are petticoats and mosquitoes where bandits are concerned?

We arrived safely, thank the Lord! Never has Trinity Church looked so good. We got a pew, but latecomers stood in the aisles. They blocked the air. It was hot and sticky. We Episcopalians kneel a lot. I began to feel woozy. Sweat puddled in the backs of my knees. Lucy Fletcher's (jumbo-sized) mother actually did faint and had to be carried outside. (Lucky her!)

Gussie helped me forget my misery. When the collection plate was passed, she reached into her pocket and took out a dime—and a matchbox. Inside the matchbox was her horny toad! Actually, it is not just her horny toad. She shares him with Gabriela, our house cook and Dovey's mama. We call Gabriela "Gabby." Gabby puts the horny toad in the kitchen window to catch flies.

I turned him on his back and tickled his tummy. He loved it. Who could be mean to such a sweet pet! When

Ray was young, he trained his horny toads to smoke cigarettes!

While the preacher was talking, Gussie tied a string around the toad's stomach and hitched him to the matchbox. He pulled his "wagon" back and forth across our laps. We muffled a giggle but Papa heard us anyway. He shifted his body a little to block Mama from spying our mischief. He's nice that way.

After dinner

Bandits are poaching our cattle! This afternoon, some of the boys found the corpses of thirty of our cattle strewn along the banks of Black Bayou. The bandits had driven the poor darlings into the quicksand. Stuck in the bog for days without food or water, the cattle died. They were then dragged out and skinned.

Chico says it's the work of Juan Cordoba, who worked at the ranch until last October. One night Chico overheard Cordoba bragging about how much money he could get for cowhides down in Mexico. Shortly afterward, Mister Ab fired him for drunkenness. Now he must be getting his revenge.

The roundup is off—for now. About three o'clock this afternoon, an armed posse left here to hunt down the murderous scoundrels. Along with Ray, Papa, our men, the sheriff and some neighbors, three young brothers, known as the Rowdy King Boys, rode all night from Seguin to join the manhunt. I imagine these boys will help hunt down the bandits and then join our roundup crew.

Monday, April 15, 1878

Papa and Ray are sleeping out in the brush tonight. Their saddles are their pillows. The sky is their blanket. May God protect them from bandits, wolves, snakes, and crawly, stinging things and bring them home safely to me.

Wednesday, April 17, 1878

The bandits have been captured! Last night, Cordoba and his band were camped by Green Lake. The Rowdy King Boys saw their campfire.

The older two Rowdies, John R. and Henry, were happy to just "tie the varmints up and let the sheriff haul 'em off to jail." But Will, the youngest, had other things in mind. He was disgusted with the way the bandits had treated our neighbors, their horses, and our cattle. He wanted to teach them a lesson. He stripped them naked, made a bonfire of their clothes, and tied each one to a thorny mesquite tree. Then he sent for the sheriff.

This Will King is something else—

Now the roundup can begin!

Thursday, April 18, 1878

Today was thrilling. You cannot imagine all the dust kicked up when the ranchers and cowboys rode off to the roundup. The horses galloped off with their riders hollering, "Yeeeeee-hawwww!" I didn't know whether to cover my eyes from the grit or my ears from the noise. It gave me goose bumps.

For days, the cowboys will live in the brush country. They're gathering cattle. In Texas, we let our cattle range free. There are no fences here. So, every spring and fall, we have to go out and find our herd before we can take them to market.

The cowboys catch one cow or steer at a time. The cattle don't make it easy. They hide under the low and tangled branches of mesquite trees. Once the cattle are caught, the cowboys make sure they are branded. Afterward, the cowboys walk them up the Chisholm Trail to Dodge City, Kansas. There they are put on a train to a Chicago meat-packing plant.

Ray always rides up the trail with the outfit (the men) and the cattle. Papa goes up to Dodge ahead of the trail drivers and arranges the sale.

The roundup makes Mister Ab feel like a dancer. "Cow work is like a ballet," he says. "Cowboys have to move and flow with the cattle."

Speaking of dance—I can't wait. It's a week from tomorrow. I think I'll wear the peach organdy. Or—should I wear the blue silk?

Saturday, April 20, 1878 (very early)

Joe One-Wing just rode in with news of the roundup. First, the good news: The brush country is crawling with cattle! The bad news is the mosquitoes. After last week's rain, the mosquitoes are swarming. At night, Joe says, the boys have to swab kerosene on their horses so they will lie down and get some rest.

"Those mosquitoes half eat us up!" said Joe. "The varmints sucked so much blood out of poor Old Paint that, when I slapped him fondly on the rump, my whole handprint was nothin' but blood."

Old Joe. He always has a great story to tell. I just never know how much of it to believe. Joe's real name is José Cantu. When he was eleven, he got his left coat sleeve caught in the gears of a windmill and lost his arm. That's why we call him Joe One-Wing.

No one out on the range has seen Ole Red—yet.

Sunday, April 21, 1878

Bedtime

Papa's home! He surprised us by riding in this evening. He says the roundup can go on without him. He wants to stay home with Mama. I haven't seen her since Easter services this morning. Papa says she's fine but Gabby whispered that she took her dinner in bed. I wonder why.

Monday, April 22, 1878

More good news from the roundup: Ole Red is captured! By the light of a full moon, Mister Ab and his men snuck up on a bunch of cattle feeding away from cover. There, grazing out in the open, was Ole Red! Mister Ab told the boys, "He's mine," and spurred his horse to corner the slippery rascal.

Ole Red saw him coming. He tossed his head, snorted, pawed the ground, and charged full speed at Mister Ab.

Mister Ab was ready. He had his lasso twirling. But his horse stepped in a gopher hole! The horse lost its balance, tripped, and threw Mister Ab onto a cactus. OUCH! There lay Mister Ab, sprawled on the ground, hurting, helpless, with seven feet of horns bearing down on him when, all of a sudden, a young cowboy galloped onto the scene. He roped Ole Red, threw him to the ground, and tied him to a tree. The brave cowboy left him to cool off until morning.

That cowboy sounds mighty brave—they say his father owns the Circle C Ranch near Beeville. The cowboy's name is Jeb Chapman.

Tuesday, April 23, 1878

Noon

Gabby, Dovey, Gussie, and I were frosting lemon cookies when we felt the rumble. It was like an earthquake. We rushed outside. Without my bonnet to shield the sun's glare, I couldn't see at first. I had to squint. To the southwest, I saw a thick cloud of dust rolling our way. The low rumble we had heard in the kitchen had, by then, become deafening thunder. Thousands of hooves pounded the earth. It was the herd running toward us. It looked like a great, brown river.

It was a wondrous sight. The roundup was done. The men were home with the cattle.

Thursday, April 25, 1878

Afternoon

Great Caesar's Ghost!!! So much change at once! First Papa tells us that Mama is going to have a baby. That is great! Then Papa tells us that, this year, he will not go to Dodge. He will stay at the ranch—with Mama. Instead, he is sending Ray to arrange for the cattle sale in Dodge. Also, he has hired Jeb Chapman to replace Ray on the trail drive. Jeb's that brave cowboy who kept Mister Ab from being gored.

I could have taken Ray's place and ridden with the cattle to Dodge! Why did Papa have to hire an outsider? By golly, I will speak to Papa tonight about Dovey and me going to Dodge.

Ole Red's been misbehaving. Ray said Jeb Chapman has put himself in charge of reforming Ole Red. Jeb tied him by the neck to one of our gentle steers named El Tuerto. If there's a steer on earth than can tame Ole Red, it's El Tuerto. He is fearless. His name means "the one-eyed." Five years ago, El Tuerto lost his eye doing battle with a Longhorn just as ornery as Ole Red.

Friday, April 26, 1878

Will wonders never cease! Papa is letting me go on the cattle drive!

I cornered Papa after supper. "With Ray in Dodge," I said to him, in my most grown-up voice, "you'll need a family member on the trail with the cowboys—to look after our cattle, of course."

Papa clapped when I was finished. "Bravo!" he said. "You'd make a great lawyer, Princess!" He confessed that he had been thinking of sending me all along. "After all," he said, "a future rancher must learn every part of the business—including the trail drive."

Dovey and I will take the buggy. Mama's having Smitty sew pockets in its doors for our personal items. Rosie's going, too. Rosie's my strawberry roan pony. She used to be a wild mustang but now she eats sugar out of my hand. Dovey even taught her to open the kitchen door with her mouth.

So much to do! I'm hardly the only one getting ready, though. From my bedroom window, I can see the cowboys preparing the wild Longhorns for the trip. We call the wild ones "outlaws." The men are moving around inside the corral, getting the outlaw cattle used to being handled. Tomorrow they'll open the gate and let the wild ones join the gentle ones grazing down by the creek. (I hope Ole Red minds his manners and doesn't have to be yoked to El Tuerto again!)

I see a bunch of new cowboys. I wonder which one is Will? Could Jeb be the tall one with the bright red bandanna? I can't wait to meet them both.

Sunday, April 28, 1878

Morning

Last night's dance was great fun. I wore my peach dress with the lace overskirt. After rinsing my hair twice in rainwater, Dovey piled it high in a bun. Into it she wove a wreath of purple and white chinaberry flowers. I smelled divine.

Every girl had to bring a cake. It was quite a juggling act to ride into town over thirteen miles of bumpy road with a double-layer, chocolate fudge cake in my lap. Surprisingly, both the cake and I arrived all in one piece.

That fiddler sure could make that fiddle talk. I do declare that I danced every waltz and polka he played. The Casino Hall was packed with lots of eligible bachelors. I was disappointed, though, that neither the Rowdy Kings nor Jeb Chapman showed up. I hear that the Rowdies are in Indianola swimming in the Gulf of Mexico. Cookie says that Jeb's back at the Circle C winding up last-minute business.

Oh, well, I guess I'll have to wait a little bit longer to get a good, long peek at the new boys. I wonder which one will be my thrill?

Monday, April 29, 1878

Note to myself:
Do not forget to pack:
- parasol
- ABC sampler to embroider for Baby Sister (I hope!)
- rifle & five boxes of cartridges
- tin plate, cup, fork, knife, spoon
- checked gingham sunbonnet
- gloves
- my best blue silk (for Dodge)
- Japanese fan
- this diary and 2 new ones, $5 worth of stamped envelopes, 2 reams of good white letter paper, & 2 bottles of ink
- lamp with durable chimney, oil, candles, matches
- my Bible & the book, *Oliver Twist*
- 2 feather mattresses & 2 rubber sheets
- tent

Tuesday, April 30, 1878
The Trail Drive Begins

I left home today. Hot tears rolled down my cheeks when Mama handed me a little square box with a label that says, "Bell Bros. Jewelers, San Antonio." I hugged her hard and tucked my present in the buggy pocket along with my diary and Bible. I'll be on the trail on July 13, my birthday. I've never been away from home on my birthday before.

The news of my going spread like wildfire. Papa's friends think he's crazy. Some rode in to talk him out of it. Others came to see us off.

It was raining again. "So much rain makes everything soggy," I griped, pulling my shawl up over my head.

Mister Ab, our trail boss, overheard me. "Oh, no, Miss Hallie," he said. "Rain makes everything grow . . . means there's a goodly amount of grass waitin' for us on up the trail."

That Mister Ab always looks on the bright side! It'll take more than a prickly pear to dampen his spirits. Despite that bad spill on the cactus (he picked out spines for days!), he's still in the saddle—with a soft pillow in it!

Gussie gave me a sweet kiss and Ray punched me in the arm. "See ya in Dodge in August," he said, winking. Papa helped Dovey and me up into the buggy. Mama and Gabby dabbed their eyes with hankies. The trail hands threw their bedrolls into the wagons and hopped on their ponies.

"Time to move out!" hollered Mister Ab. The wagons led the way. Cookie climbed into the chuck wagon and cracked his whip above the heads of the mules. Next rolled Joe One-Wing in the supply wagon. With Dovey at the reins, our buggy fell in third.

Chico unmuffled the brass bells on the lead steer, El Tuerto, and the bell cow, Mrs. Bubbies. Once their bells were cleared, they moved to their regular spots. El Tuerto walked his way through the herd to the front. The scattered cattle looked for him and heard the bell. They bawled their heads off and fell in behind. Mrs. Bubbies went the opposite direction—to the end of the line. She always walks at the rear with the "little dogies," the poor dear orphan yearlings. She's their babysitter.

The men who are the trail hands then surrounded the herd. Mister Ab, his new assistant, Jeb, and their dogs galloped to the front. (Jeb IS the tall one with the bright red bandanna!) The three Rowdies and a tenderfoot named Little Rusty took their places on the left and right of the herd. Pulling up the rear trotted two negro tenderfoots, Bud and Ed. They'd tied bandannas over their noses and mouths. It's dusty at the back. Behind them rode Chico with his string of cow ponies.

Mister Ab shouted over his shoulder to the slow cows in the rear, "Get along, little dogies!" We were bound for Dodge!

It was a bittersweet moment—with the chocolate trail unwinding before me and all the waving people growing smaller and smaller behind me at the ranch—

Thursday, May 2, 1878
North of Cuero, Texas

Morning

The last thing I thought I'd get on this trail drive was a lecture. Cookie woke us up yelling, "Come and git it! Come a-running, boys—er—and girls!" After we had gathered around the fire for coffee, Cookie told us his rules. No peeking in his pots and pans. Don't ride or walk too close to the fire and kick up dirt around the food. Serve yourself.

What a bossy britches. Even the boss man, Mister Ab, has to mind Cookie's rules. Who's really running this outfit—Mister Ab or Cookie?

Gabby would have shook her wooden spoon at him and said "Tsk, tsk!" to see what Cookie calls "breakfast." Black kind of sums up what he placed in front of us this morning. The mesquite-burnt venison was blackened to a crisp . . . and the bread! It was almost black from the swarms of mosquitoes that landed in the rising dough and got stuck. I closed my eyes and ate it anyway.

Jeb and his big dog, Dooley, are working with the outlaw bull, Ole Red, so he doesn't stampede the herd. Jeb draped a loop over his horns and led him around camp. If even once he stepped out of line, Dooley barked and bit at his shins.

We're moving at a brisk pace—about twenty miles a day. This tires the animals and makes them tamer. We sleep under the pecan trees and keep our wagons pointed at the North Star.

Friday, May 3
Outside Gonzales, Texas, on the Guadalupe River

Dusk

Bread, meat, beans, and coffee. That's what we have every day, three times a day. The biscuits are rubber, the meat is tree bark, the beans are rocks, and the coffee is turpentine. Well, at least we eat civilized, thanks to "the Preacher." That's what we call John R. King. I wish you could have seen how red his face got when Chico recited his favorite cowboy grace today at lunch:

> Eat the meat and leave the skin;
>   Turn up your plate and let's dig in.

Golly, was John R. mad! We bowed our head as he said a "proper grace." Then he made us all wash up. "Cleanliness is next to godliness," he barked. Half of what he says is conversation. The other half is quotes from the Bible to back up what he said in the first half.

I know now why he and his two brothers are called the Rowdy King Boys. They like a good time. Even the Preacher is fun-loving. The three of them played a trick on Cookie today.

We had stopped for lunch on Peach Creek. After eating, Cookie sat on the root of a big tree facing the creek and fell asleep. Will threw a log in the river just in front of the sleeping Cookie. On cue, John R. and Henry shouted, "Alligator!"

In a quick effort to get up, Cookie, instead, slipped into the river, went under, and came up beside the floating log, which he thought was the alligator. He screamed, "Help!" Henry quickly tossed him a rope. Once he made it to the riverbank, Cookie was mortified to discover that he had only escaped from a rotting log. He wandered off into the woods to sulk. A bit later, he slunk quietly back into camp toting an armful of wood.

Will has a merry twinkle in his eye and dimples in both cheeks. When he smiles, I melt.

Saturday, May 4, 1878
Still outside Gonzales, Texas

Afternoon

Cookie is covered with red blotches. I think he got into some poison oak yesterday fetching that firewood. I figured that cream of tartar mixed with sulphur and salts would stop his itching. I had everything but the sulphur. Chico saddled up Rosie for me and, this morning, Dovey and I rode into Gonzales to find a pharmacy.

In Gonzales, the streets were bustling with people. For some reason, they all seemed to be heading for the courthouse. It wasn't hard to find the pharmacy. A big sign hung over the door, H.L. Beaumont, Druggist & Chemist. But, unfortunately, another sign was hung on the door announcing that it was closed. All the other stores we passed were also closed. That seemed odd, it being a Saturday and the town so crammed with shoppers.

We soon found out what was going on. A man was being hanged in front of the jail. People had come from all over the countryside to watch. When we rode up, the executioner was just bringing the prisoner up the steps to the platform. The prisoner was handcuffed and seemed very defiant. We got down off our horses and tied them to a rail. We joined the crowd standing behind a high fence just a few feet away from the platform.

Other men were standing on the platform. The prisoner turned to an older man among them and said, "Do you believe I killed your son, Brother?"

To which the older man replied, "I do!"

"You believe a doggone lie!" said the prisoner. "I didn't do it! It was my blasted brother-in-law, John Wesley Hardin!"

The executioner ignored his statement of innocence and slipped the black cap over the condemned man's head. Then he placed the noose on his neck. He released the trap door. Dovey hid her head in her hands, but I watched. I saw the prisoner drop through the trap door, and I heard his neck snap. Back and forth, his limp body swung lifelessly from the gallows.

By the time we returned to the pharmacy, the shop was open. I overheard some customers whisper the name of the executed man: Brown Bowen. A jury had convicted Bowen of killing a man named Thomas Holderman. Was Bowen really guilty, though, or did his brother-in-law, John Wesley Hardin, commit the murder, as Bowen had claimed before he was hanged?

We bought our medicine and headed back to camp. Dovey and I were both badly shaken. On our way back, I tore the bustle off my green wool riding outfit and tossed it into some bushes. Such a silly thing to wear in such a serious place—

Sunday, May 5, 1878
Leaving Gonzales, Texas

Pre-dawn

The tinkling of El Tuerto's bell awakened me. Chico has just brought in some fresh horses for the next shift. The lead steer, El Tuerto, "the one-eyed," is with them. He's so spoiled. The cowboys treat him like a pet. Right now El Tuerto's prowling around the pots and pans looking for scraps of meat and biscuits. Cookie doesn't make the special lead steer follow his rules. Mister Ab positively dotes on him. He feeds him shelled corn and prunes and lets him lick the skillets!

Cookie's rash is better—but the Rowdies are in deep pain. I don't think they'll be playing any tricks on Cookie any time soon. He fixed that, for sure. While Dovey and I were in Gonzales, Cookie made up a big pot of chili and served it to the boys. Secretly, he put way too much pepper in it. Now the Rowdies' mouths are on fire. Will's walking around sucking on a wet washcloth.

Something wonderful happened last night. The hem of my riding habit dragged in the campfire and caught fire. It burned off several inches of hemline. Now the dress is a better length for walking around. Before, it caught cockleburs that cut up my ankles. Mama would frown to see my ankles peeking out from my skirt, but at least they won't bleed any more.

Tuesday, May 7, 1878
On San Marcos River, south of Luling, Texas

Ah, this is the life! Neither Dovey nor I had to drive the buggy today. My two brown ponies have gotten the rhythm of the trail. They just follow the slow-moving herd. Today, I fastened the reins, leaned back into my seat, and sewed while the ponies pulled my buggy across Central Texas.

Wednesday, May 8, 1878
South of Lockhart, Texas, on the Clear Fork
of Plum Creek

Afternoon

Our troubles began last night. Just after sundown, Mister Ab bedded down the herd. The cows had just dozed off when the young trail hand Little Rusty let out a big, "Ker—chew!" The sneeze spooked the cattle and they stampeded. They ran into the woods and scattered. Ever since then, Jeb, Will, and Mister Ab have been trying to round up the thirty that are missing. We haven't seen those men since they left last night. They didn't come in for breakfast. I guess they slept in the saddle. I hope they're all right.

We're waiting for them to return. Dovey and I are cross-eyed from too much cross-stitching. While I was sitting here writing, Dovey pitched a great idea. "Let's go fishing!" she suggested. She's grabbing the tackle box and we're heading for the creek. Jeb's dog, Dooley, has taken a liking to me. He's going fishing with us.

I asked Cookie if he had ever heard of a man named John Wesley Hardin. I told him what the condemned man had said before he was hanged in Gonzales.

"Sure, I've heard of John Wesley Hardin. Who hasn't? Hardin's killed more men than I can count on my two hands," said Cookie. "He's a dangerous scamp. The Texas Rangers finally nabbed him in Florida, I hear. He's in jail right now for killing another man named Webb."

What if Hardin did indeed kill Holderman? If he did, then that poor man in Gonzales was executed for a crime he didn't commit.

Early evening

Thank heavens! All the men and cattle are back—including, the outlaw bull, Ole Red. Jeb chased him all night and half the day trying to turn him toward camp. But Ole Red kept stampeding. Jeb even tossed dirt in his eyes, but still Ole Red wouldn't turn. Finally, Jeb fired his six-shooter near that ornery bull's "tender parts." That did the trick. Jeb hog-tied him overnight to make him think about his bad behavior.

Dovey and I surprised the men with a special supper of pan-fried catfish and roasted potatoes. "This food tastes mighty good, Miss Hallie," said Jeb, tipping his hat in my direction, yet keeping his eyes firmly on the ground. (I think he's the strong, silent type.)

Jeb's terribly shy—just the opposite of Will. Today, for example, Will picked a buttercup for me to smell. When I leaned forward, he dusted my nose with the flower! I looked a sight—all covered in yellow pollen!

Saturday, May 11, 1878
Northeast of Austin, Texas, at Wilbarger Creek

Evening

We trailed the herd seventeen miles today. The rolling green pastures of Central Texas sure are pretty but they do make for a bumpy buggy ride. My shawl has found new service as a seat cushion. My bottom is one big bruise!

We crossed both Onion Creek and the Colorado River fine. Mister Ab was worried about taking the cattle through both crossings, particularly the Colorado, which has rapids. But Mister Ab knows this trail like the back of his hand. He led us to a ford a few miles south of Austin near Montopolis.

Just when we thought the herd was under control, a train came barreling out of the east, belching black smoke. The engineer blew his whistle and the cattle "went on the prod" (stampeded)! That Jeb is quick, though! He rode into the cattle and got them to turn so that they were running in a circle. They got so tired, milling and milling and getting nowhere, that they soon settled down and minded the trail hands.

Mister Ab said to Jeb, "Good work, Bolivar!" (He calls everyone "Bolivar.") That's high praise from Mister Ab. He says a good cowboy is "more than a man with guts and a horse who can rope like a wizard and ride anything that wears hair. A real, top hand buckaroo," he says, "has to have cow sense—a gift."

We made it to Wilbarger Creek before dark.

Sunday, May 12, 1878
Northeast of Austin, Texas, at Wilbarger Creek

Late at night

This was a golden day. I want to write about it before the memory fades. Already the lamplight grows dim—

Today we didn't travel. It was a true Sabbath, a day of rest for all of us—except for Mrs. Bubbies, our bell cow. She gave birth to two heifers this morning. When we resume travel, Joe One-Wing will toss her new calves into the supply wagon with the other calves born on the trail. He'll put loose sacks on them so that their scents won't get mixed up with the other calves as they jostle along the trail. In that way, Mrs. Bubbies will recognize her babies and give them milk every evening when we break for camp.

We're starting to feel like a family. Tonight, after dinner, the off-duty cowboys hung their saddles in the low live oak branches and spread bedding for us to sit on. We sat around the campfire. Even grumpy Cookie got in the mood and passed around tin plates of "bread and lick" (molasses). John R. read a Bible passage to the group. Will and Henry serenaded us with banjo and fife. Jeb played "Get Along, Little Dogies" on his harmonica. Will took my hand and we danced a slow waltz. The cattle loved the music. They made a soft lowing sound. It was like a big city symphony! We all wanted to laugh, but that would have made those crazy cattle stampede for sure.

Joe One-Wing told a scary story. We're camped beside Wilbarger Creek, named for a brave pioneer named Josiah Wilbarger. Just a few miles from here, Josiah was attacked by Comanches and scalped. The Indians left him for dead.

The Indians were mistaken, though. Josiah was not dead. He managed to drag himself to some springs, drink, and bathe his aching head. With his fingernails, he dug until he found some snails to eat. Then he crawled over to a live oak and collapsed.

Around midnight, he heard a soft voice calling his name. He awoke to see his dear sister, Margaret, walking toward him.

"Josiah," she said, "Do not fear." She pointed to the southeast. "Help will come to you from this direction." Then she vanished into thin air.

At that very same moment, six miles to the southeast, Sarah Hornsby, was having the strangest dream. She dreamed she saw her neighbor, Josiah Wilbarger, leaning against an oak tree, soaked in blood and dying. She got out of bed, awakened her husband, Reuben, and told him her incredible vision. Reuben immediately organized a search party.

Amazingly, the men found Josiah exactly where Sarah had said. They took him home and nursed him back to health.

Slowly, Josiah began to recover from his many injuries. Three months passed. One day, a letter arrived for him from Missouri. The letter told him that his sister, Margaret, had died. The mail had been very slow.

Margaret had died three months before. She had died the very night she had appeared to Josiah at midnight. It had been Margaret's spirit that gave Sarah Hornsby the marvelous dream that saved her brother.

Monday, May 13, 1878
Still at Wilbarger Creek, Texas

Evening

Ray told me I'd see wild animals on this trip— buffalo, elk, antelope, deer. "Perhaps you'll spot a wolf or even a bear," he had said. But he never said anything about a camel!

It all started after breakfast, when Mister Ab announced we were staying in camp another day. "This grass is ten inches tall here, and as green as a wheat field," he said. "It's too good to pass up."

Dovey and I were glad. We needed a washday. After gathering our dirty (and odoriferous) laundry, we walked to a private spot a long way from camp. After all, a lady does not air her undergarments in public! We rinsed our clothes in the creek.

As I was draping my corset over a bush to dry, I heard a snort. I looked up to see nine camels drinking a few feet from us downstream. As soon as the camels smelled me, they popped their lips, and snorted some more.

I was afraid they'd bolt before we got a good look at them. Dovey and I ran to introduce ourselves to the camel drover, Mr. Lansfear. He said his camels are descendents of the ones that carried U.S. Army supplies from Texas to California. He commanded one camel to kneel down on her knobby knees, and Dovey and I got on. Her saddle blanket was sewn with little flashing mirrors and bells jingled from her two humps. At first, I felt like Cleopatra of the Nile. That lasted about two seconds. All that rocking motion made me feel so vomity. I got down. I think I'll stick to riding Rosie.

When the camel caravan got lined up to leave, Mr. Lansfear led them in the opposite direction of our herd. "If your cattle get a whiff of my camels, they'll stampede. Even the horses will try to escape," he said. "I've seen horses climb trees when they smell a camel!"

He says a camel has such a powerful odor that a horse can smell it three miles away. That I can believe. I've scrubbed my hands raw with lye soap and I still can't shake their musty smell!

Thursday, May 16, 1878
Arrive at the San Gabriel River, Texas

What a hot day. It's made us so sluggish. We only covered twelve miles today. When we finally reached the San Gabriel River, we found it swift and rising by the hour. It must be raining to the north of us. We couldn't make the cattle swim to the other side. Finally, after three hours of urging them across, we gave up and bedded them down on the south bank. It's dangerous to wait to cross. By morning, the river could be even higher. But what else could we do? Carry the cattle across on our shoulders?

It was dark when we sat down near the chuck wagon and Cookie served us supper. We were all tired and hungry. Little Rusty came up to Dovey and me and offered to pitch our tent and spread our bedding for us. I think he has a crush on us. I thanked him kindly and he went to work.

Friday, May 17, 1878
Cross San Gabriel, Texas

Morning

My hand is trembling. I have never been so frightened in my life. And to think that I almost lost Dovey—

I didn't sleep a wink last night. Dovey and I fell asleep as usual, sharing our double bedroll. Remember, Little Rusty spread the bedding for us. All night long, I tossed and turned. Something was poking me in the ribs. I thought it was Dovey's elbows.

I don't know how, with all that poking going on, but I finally fell asleep. The next thing I knew, Jeb's dog, Dooley, was standing over me. He was licking my face and whining. He wouldn't stop. He wanted me to get up. I was afraid he'd start barking and spook the cattle. I got up and walked outside with him. That seemed to please him. He stopped whining and parked himself in front of our tent. By that point, I was wide awake. I grabbed my lantern, found my copy of *Oliver Twist,* and wandered over to the fire to read.

Soon, a light rain began to fall. I wanted to go back inside my tent. But Dooley wouldn't let me. Each time

50

I stepped closer to the doorway, he snapped and snarled some more.

Jeb must have heard all the fuss because he came over to see what was happening. When Dooley saw his master, he went crazy. He jumped on him and then ran back into the tent, standing over the blankets and barking like mad. Jeb shone his lamp into the tent. By this time, Dovey was awake and sitting up. My side of the bed was, of course, empty.

Dooley still stood on my side, barking at some hump in the middle under my side of the blankets. Something was in there. An enormous ridge ran from my pillow to the foot of the bed. It looked like a fallen oak branch.

I laughed. So that's what had been "elbowing" me— a tree limb. Little Rusty had foolishly spread our blankets on top of it. I'd tease him later. I reached out to roll back the blankets and remove it.

Instantly, Dooley sprung in my path. He set his teeth in my sleeve and growled. I released the blanket and backed up. Jeb laid a gentle hand on my shoulder. "Please step outside, Miss Hallie." He motioned for Dovey to do the same.

Dovey and I watched from the doorway as Jeb threw back the blankets. Underneath our covers lay a six-foot rattlesnake! Little Rusty must have laid our blankets over his hole. In the night, he had crawled out and snuggled up between Dovey and me!

The rattlesnake began to crawl. Jeb raised his rifle. Would he shoot? If he did, the cattle would stampede. If he didn't, the snake might kill both him and Dooley. What was he to do?

Then Dooley began to circle that big snake. He walked around and around it, barking furiously while the snake coiled and rattled and tried to strike. This went on and on until I thought it never would stop and Dooley would get bitten and his head would swell then he would die or Jeb would die or the cattle would stampede, when suddenly Dooley lunged at the awful snake and sank his teeth in behind its mean head. That dog shook that snake so hard that it broke apart in three different pieces.

Jeb cut off the snake's rattles—all eighteen—and strung them on a leather collar for Dooley to wear. Now he jingles when he walks. Cookie fried up the rattlesnake for the dogs—

I made myself a new promise I know I can keep. From now on, no matter how tired I am, I'm spreading my own blankets—

Arrive Willis Creek, Texas

Evening

Dovey and I were down by the creek picking dewberries when we heard a scream. It was Little Rusty. He was over in a clearing about a hundred feet away from us.

"Hey, ladies, look what I found!" he shouted at us. Once he got our attention, he reached inside a stump and held up something black and small.

"There's three of 'em," he yelled, "three of the darlingest kittens you've ever seen! And they ain't even got their eyes open yet!"

Dovey and I dropped our pails. Kittens! We love kittens. We tried to scramble up the riverbank, but the slope was wet and we couldn't get a foothold. We kept running up and slipping back. We were stuck. It turned out to have been a good thing the riverbank was so muddy because, just then, we heard a second scream.

"Mercy me, she got me!" Little Rusty was running straight for the creek, with a mad Mama Skunk chasing him. Those were no ordinary kittens! Those were polecats!

Little Rusty dove into the creek, clothes and all. He washed and washed and splashed and splashed and rubbed and rubbed, but it didn't make a bit of difference. That Mama Skunk had sprayed him well. He stunk to high heaven. Little Rusty walked back into camp. Mister Ab ordered him to take off his smelly clothes and carry them on a stick to the creek and bury them. Those were his only clothes. Now he's wearing Mister Ab's big trousers tied up with horse rope. He looks so funny.

Who am I, though, to poke fun at appearances? I look like a glorified rainbow. My dress is covered in orange mud and my lips and hands are stained purplish-red from dewberry picking (and dewberry nibbling! YUM!).

Saturday, May 18, 1878
Arrive Little River, Texas

Cookie woke us with, "Rise and shine! Grub pile!" He was whistling and singing and laughing. He served us dewberry flapjacks for breakfast. With a skillet in each hand, he can flip two flapjacks at the same time!

His flapjacks were delicious—brown and fluffy with sweet, crunchy berries inside. He actually apologized to us for not having any cold, fresh milk to wash them down with! (Longhorns aren't milk cows.)

I'd never seen him so nice. He's usually so grumpy. I guess Dovey gave him those dewberries. I wonder if she also picked the pretty wildflowers sitting on the lid of his chuckbox?

It's still sprinkling. The cattle wouldn't settle down to sleep last night. They kept walking after nightfall and we had to follow. It's easier to keep them together now that we're on the open prairie. We finally made camp at 11:00 P.M. and had another cold dinner of beef jerky and cornpone (we're out of wheat flour).

Monday, May 20, 1878
At Temple, Texas

Noon

It's drizzling. We stopped here, hoping for a hot lunch. But Cookie couldn't keep the campfire lit. The rain kept putting it out. Dovey tried to help him by holding my parasol over the stack of wood while

Cookie struck the matches. But the fire kept sputtering and dying out. There's nothing to eat but stale crackers and raw bacon. That makes the cowboys really cranky.

Jeb loaned me his rain slicker to keep my dress dry.

Midnight

It's still drizzling and the wind is up. It makes the cattle walk and walk—even in the dark. What can we do but follow? Mister Ab just now got the cattle bedded down for the night and we made camp. Everybody is wet, tired, hungry, and grouchy. What I wouldn't do for a roof over my head, a hot bath, and a comfortable bed!

Wednesday, May 22, 1878
About 20 miles north of Temple, Texas

Mid-morning

Last night was the scariest night of my life. It's a miracle we're still alive.

How can I begin to describe such a terrifying storm? We knew we were in big trouble yesterday at noon. As we ate our lunch, gray, puffy clouds swirled low over our heads. By sundown, the sky had turned an ugly black, with mean streaks of yellow and green.

At supper, Joe One-Wing put the fear of God in us. He looked up at the dark sky and said, "Looks like a Texas twister's a-comin'!" He claimed to have once ridden out a tornado chained to a stump. "That mean old wind picked me up and flopped me against the ground," he said, "but I hung on for dear life!"

We looked for a safe place to camp—a high hill or a patch of timber. But for miles in every direction, there was nothing but flat prairie. We were forced to camp out in the open.

Dovey and I were in our beds when we heard the first growl of distant thunder. Next came the rain—soft and gentle, at first. It went pitter-patter against our tent. We snuggled closer.

Then the wind began to blow. It picked up speed. It howled and beat against our tent walls. Rain poured down. Thunder crackled and shook the very ground we slept on. Lightning flashed. Water seeped beneath our tent. Our beds started floating. We were sure we would drown.

We were doomed. Dovey and I recited the Twenty-third Psalm. "Yea, though I walk through the valley of the shadow of death, I will fear no evil. . . ."

Then everything went dark. A big gust of wind had blown out our candle. I fumbled for the matches but they were soaked. Then an even bigger gust hit, knocking our tent down on top of us.

The next thing I knew, Jeb was lifting the tent off us. He had seen our light go out. With him guiding us, we dashed through the driving rain for the safety of the chuck wagon.

Once we were settled inside, Jeb made the strangest request.

"Would you ladies be so kind as to take out your metal hairpins?" he asked. "This air is charged with electricity," he explained. "You never know what a freaky Texas storm will do." I couldn't help noticing that he stared at my hair as Dovey let it down. Did he think it was pretty? I was relieved to see he had taken off his spurs and his pistol.

Forked lightning lit up the night sky, so we could see Jeb ride off. The lighting was dazzling. It lit up the prairie. Hundreds of cattle were scattered across it. Our cowboys on horseback were trying desperately to keep them from stampeding. Everything was electrified!

Lightning zigzagged back and forth across the cows' horns! It buzzed across the brims of the cowboys' hats and the tips of the horses' ears! The air smelled of burning sulphur. It got so hot with electricity, I almost fainted.

The storm raged all night. We were safe and dry inside the chuck wagon for a spell. But then a big wind came and blew the top off. Chunks of hail pelted us as we dashed for cover under the wagon. The noise of hail and rain and thunder was so terrible that I cupped my hands over my ears. I thought I'd go crazy from that incessant noise. Never, though, did I hear the most terrible sound of all—the sound of two thousand cattle stampeding. How on earth were the men holding the cattle? Was I imagining it or did I really hear Jeb's harmonica above all the clatter? Dovey and I huddled together and cried for daylight.

Morning brought a golden sun and a big blue sky. Rain had washed the leaves of the oaks all green and glossy. Amid such beauty, it was hard to believe we had passed such an ugly night.

Our campsite was a soggy mess. All around, holes were gouged out in the earth, like bombs had been dropped. "Lightning does that," said Jeb, helping Cookie put the canvas top back on his chuck wagon.

Poor Jeb! He was soaked to the bone! No wonder—I still have his rain slicker! How stupid of me not to have returned it!

Five of our cattle were struck dead by lighting. Poor Little Rusty had forgotten to take off his spurs and was hit, too. He was badly burned. Bud and Ed had blood blisters on their hands and shoulders from the hail. When Will saw me salving and bandaging their hands, he pretended to have blisters, too. He just wanted me to hold his hand, I think.

Mister Ab slapped Jeb on the back and said, "You're a top hand buckaroo, Bolivar!" According to Joe, while I had been safe and dry all night, Jeb had ridden around the herd (without a slicker) on his night horse. He had played his harmonica and sung his songs—long and lonesome songs, timed to a slow walk—to soothe the cattle. As a result, the herd didn't stampede. They had stayed calm—including that former rebel rouser, Ole Red. Quite a triumph for Jeb and the others!

Thanks to Smitty, my diary is nice and dry. It rode out the storm snug in the buggy pocket—along with that birthday box I am dying to open! I made a big production of showing everyone in camp that they were dry. Smitty is such a fine craftsman!

I turn fifteen on July 13. Jeb says we'll be in Indian Territory then—

Sunday, May 26, 1878
On Childress Creek, northwest of Waco, Texas

We're having a horrible time finding grass in these hills. The mama cows aren't eating enough grass to make milk for their calves. Today, Jeb rode on ahead and spotted a green pasture off the trail. When we took our herd there to graze, settlers came at us with shotguns. They ordered us off their land. Now we have to keep to the trail.

A strange and unexpected thing has happened. Ole Red has moved his position in the herd. He's walking up front with El Tuerto, leading the herd. He's being cooperative, too. Will wonders never cease? Good work, Jeb.

Monday, May 27, 1878
At King Creek, Texas

Late

The night is clear. I can see both the Big and Little Dippers from the opening in my tent.

Last night we had one of the biggest stampedes of the entire trip. A wolf got in with the herd and made them run. The night watch lost a whole night's sleep. We've got to find these cattle some grass or we'll have even more stampedes. "A cow with its fill of grass and water is less likely to stampede," says Mister Ab. If these cattle go two more days with no grass, we'll have nothing but cow skin and cow bones to sell in Dodge.

The wolves are howling. They're watching us. Earlier, they tried to slink close to camp. We could see their yellow eyes. So Cookie built the fire higher. It will burn all night.

The boys are up later than usual. They are sitting around the fire, playing cards and whittling sticks. In the distance, one of the cowboys on night watch is singing, "Bury me not on the lone prairie." Hearing cards shuffling, boys singing, and spurs jingling makes me feel safe enough to close my eyes.

Friday, May 31, 1878
At the Brazos River at Kimball, Texas

We've been waiting three days to cross this swollen river. It looks like the water might finally be going down a little. Maybe we can cross in the morning. Fifteen other herds are camped nearby, also waiting to cross. Meanwhile, our herd is eating its fill of grass.

It feels like summer, it's so hot and muggy. Rain's given us a big crop of mosquitoes. I'll never finish sewing this sampler for my new baby sister! Not if I have to stop every second to swat a mosquito with my broomweed switch!

The Rowdies hung some tarps between the wagon tops to give us shade for our sewing. Dovey slit my green wool skirt straight down the middle and is making me a pair of trousers. John R. disapproves. He quoted from the Book of Deuteronomy: "The woman shall not wear that which pertaineth unto a man." He is so narrow-minded! How would he like to wear a dress on a cattle drive? Dresses drag the ground. The one I'm wearing is caked with mud. And he was the one who said cleanliness is next to godliness!

Cookie sure is in a good mood these days. Because we're low on food, he butchered a lame steer. He cut up the beef into chunks and dried most of it for jerky. With the rest, he made a delicious son-of-a-gun stew. What a treat! I noticed that Dovey carried the wooden washtub of dirty dishes down to the river after the meal and Cookie ran to help her. I heard them laughing. Together they dipped the plates in the muddy red water, rubbed them with sand, rinsed them, and laid them on the riverbank to dry. They seem so happy.

I got up the courage to speak to Jeb yesterday evening. He says so little. I knew it would be up to me to start a conversation if we were to ever have one. He was out in the pasture where the cattle were grazing. He moved among them like a doctor, checking them for disease. I wandered over and asked him why he had come on this trip. After all, I pointed out, he was really a rancher, not a trail hand. (Since when does the future owner of the Circle C Ranch need to earn $50 a month as a straw boss? I thought to myself.)

He paused before replying. "Aw, shucks, Miss Hallie," he said, looking right at me for the very first time, "I can't rightly say. All I know is that it just doesn't get any better than this—just ridin' horses and ropin' calves." With that said, he politely tipped his hat and returned to his cow work.

How can such a serious boy have such dreamy blue eyes?

Monday, June 3, 1878
Arrive Fort Worth, Texas

We made it to the big city of Fort Worth. I've never seen so many cowboys! Now I know why they call Fort Worth "Cowtown." Cowboys have ridden in from north, south, east, and west to take a break from the trail. They've bedded their herds outside of town and taken the day off. Mister Ab divided our outfit into two shifts and gave each trail hand a half a day off in town. Mister Ab sold the drag yearlings and the lame cattle to some northern beef buyers for fifty cents a head—a fair price.

This town is wild and woolly. It's full of all sorts of desperate characters. Tacked up on every wall is a "wanted" poster for a bad man named Sam Bass. According to the poster, earlier this spring, he and his band held up four trains just forty miles east of here. They say Fort Worth is his hideout. Sure enough, Fort Worth is no place for a lady.

Women do live in this town but they're painted women, floozies, not the sort a man would take home to meet his mother.

After checking into a hotel, our group split up. From our second-floor room, I spied Little Rusty pushing through the swinging doors of Tom Prindle's Saloon across the street. The Rowdies walked into the barbershop to get their handlebar mustaches and goatees trimmed. Cookie headed straight for the grocery to stock up on food for the five-hundred-mile drive to Dodge. Mister Ab's checking the mail for us. I haven't seen Jeb or the rest of the fellows.

After doing some shopping, Dovey and I will have our fortunes told by a palmist named Madame Henry.

Tuesday, June 4, 1878
In Fort Worth, Texas

Morning

It is so nice to have money to spend! Dovey and I found the greatest little general store here, B. C. Evans Dry Goods. It has everything our little hearts desire. The old me would have headed straight for the bolts of satin, silk, and lace. But not Chisholm Trail Hallie! Calicos and cottons are the only thing for the trail.

I tried to wear that divided skirt Dovey sewed for me, but it just wouldn't do. Wool is too hot! And, besides, the legs of the skirt are so full that they get tangled up in the saddlehorn. I bought a pair of trousers just like the boys'. They're black cotton with a white stripe up the sides. I got a whole cowboy outfit—a navy blue hickory shirt with a shield on the front, a red bandanna, a Stetson hat, gauntlet gloves, boots, spurs, and a saddle with the prong in the middle! Riding side-saddle is banished forever! On the trail, comfort and practicality are the name of the game.

Since I'll be riding Rosie more and be in the buggy less, I won't have my trusty rifle beside me. So I bought a pearl-handled pistol with a hip holster. I also bought the newest issue of Godey's Lady's Book and a Montgomery Ward catalog plus some saltwater taffy. I restocked my medicine bag.

Later

Something terrible has happened. Little Rusty's dead. He was in the wrong place at the wrong time. He was playing poker over in the saloon. While he was dealing a hand of blackjack, a badman rode inside the bar on his horse. He pulled out his gun and killed the bartender. Then everyone in the place pulled out his gun and began shooting. It was a real-life barroom brawl! A stray bullet clipped Little Rusty in the left temple. The undertaker is making him a pine coffin. Mr. Ab's sending the body to Rusty's mama in San Antonio. Poor Little Rusty. He never did have any luck but bad.

Some oily character named Butch Craven signed on to take Little Rusty's place. He's no cowboy, if I'm any judge of character. He reeks of whiskey. His hands are like a baby's hands—soft and white—not rough and callused like a man who runs cattle. An expensive gold watch hangs from a chain in his vest pocket. How'd he afford that? And his hair—that couldn't be his natural color. It's way too dark. I think he puts shoe black on it because I noticed something black on his hands after he ran them through his hair. Mighty suspicious, if you ask me.

He's no gentleman, either. When he was introduced to me, he leered at me, winked, bent over, and kissed my hand. A cowboy doesn't do that. A cowboy bows politely and tips his hat. A cowboy may be full of devilment. He may be crude. He may dunk his doughnuts and gulp his grub and pick his teeth and scratch his backside in public. He may stretch the truth a mile just to get a laugh. But a cowboy always treats a lady decently.

As long as Butch is with us, I'm sleeping with one eye open.

Oh, I got a letter from home. China Doll's going to have kittens! Oh, how I hope she'll let me come near them.

I haven't stopped thinking about what Madame Henry said when I asked her if she saw any men in my future. She took my right hand and turned it over to reveal its palm. With her fat fingers, she traced my lifeline.

"Still waters run deep," she said, three times in a row. Hmmm. . . . What could she have meant?

Thursday, June 6, 1878
At Elizabeth Creek, Texas

Evening

Summer is both bad and good. It's bad because it's so blasted hot. It's good because the days are longer.

Summer means more sunlight after supper to write in my diary. Lamplight is so weak. It makes my eyes sting.

Sewing my alphabet sampler by this crystal clear creek named Elizabeth made me think: What if Mama named my baby sister-to-be Elizabeth? Then I could call her a billion jillion different names—Bette or Betsy or Bitsy or Lisa or Liz or Lizzie or Liza or Eliza or Lilibet or Lili or Ellie or Ella or even Elizabeth—

We just passed a trail outfit returning from Dodge. They reported that the Chisholm Trail is closed up ahead at Red River Station. There's no inspector. We'll have to change course. We must veer northwest and cross the Red River at Doan's Crossing where there is an inspector. That means trailing our cattle through the Western Cross Timbers. We could lose track of our herd in the woods. Right now, the grazing is good— we're moving at about nine miles a day. Too bad we have to leave the open prairie.

Dovey's riding up front with Cookie in the chuck-wagon. They make a sweet couple. I wonder if they are thinking of marriage. Dovey's mother, Gabby, got married at fifteen.

My horses are pulling the buggy by themselves at the back of the herd with Chico and the remuda (horses). I'm riding Rosie in front of the herd. The men said not a word when they first saw me in my new "duds" yesterday. Everything I am wearing is too big, but who cares! I cinched up my trousers with a sash and tied my hat on with a scarf. My leather gloves are roomy enough for twenty fingers but I just adore their fringed sides. When I ride, my sash, scarf, and fringe fly out behind me and flap in the wind! I feel free as a bird! Riding up front with El Tuerto, Ole Red, Mister Ab, and Jeb, I turn in my saddle and look back. The entire face of the earth is a moving mass of heads and horns.

Friday, June 7, 1878
At Oliver Creek, Texas

We waved good-bye to civilization when we left Fort Worth. Hardly anyone lives in this desolate stretch of North Texas. It's too close to the Indian Territory. Years before, Comanches ran off any pioneers foolhardy enough to come here. Over the last two days, we've passed scores of burned cabins, empty barns, and abandoned wheat fields. We've seen only one settler— an old woman. She was sitting on the front porch of her log cabin in a broken-down rocking chair, stringing beans. Three chickens squawked around her feet.

I rode up to chat with her. She lived by herself, she said. I asked her if she ever got lonely so far away from other people.

"Lonely?" she asked. "Why should I get lonely? I've got my chickens, don't I?" She explained how, one day, a neighbor had brought her the chickens in an old gunnysack.

I enjoyed visiting with her so much that I lost track of time. I looked up to see the herd a good mile down the trail. I needed to catch up. I bid the old woman a hasty farewell and hurriedly mounted my horse. As I rode off, I heard her say something. Thinking she was speaking to me, I looked back. But she was only talking to her chickens. She was telling them how much they needed a good rain.

Dovey found a stray milk cow in a patch of woods. She named her Elsie. After hobbling her, she milked her. Cookie was thrilled. He put the three pints of milk in a covered pail under the chuck wagon. Tomorrow we'll have sweet cream for our coffee.

Sunday, June 9, 1878
At Decatur, Texas

Good old Dovey! She's like a tonic to Cookie! The happier he is, the tastier our meals! For breakfast today, Cookie made fluffy biscuits—not at all like the rubbery clods he used to serve us. And we had fresh butter to slather on the piping hot rolls. Yesterday, before we hit the trail, Dovey had milked Elsie and then put the milk churn under the chuck wagon. All day long, the wagon had jolted along the trail. By the end of the day, that milk had turned into butter.

I told you so! That Butch Craven is bad news. Yesterday, about mid-afternoon, Mister Ab sent him into the woods to gather firewood. (We have to take advantage of all this wood here in the Cross Timbers. Soon we'll be on the Rolling Plains with no trees for fuel.) Later, as we rode into the Decatur city limits, the sheriff stopped us. He asked to speak to our trail boss. He accused Mister Ab of harboring a thief. A settler, he said, had spotted one of our cowboys stealing his fence railings. Mister Ab told the sheriff he must have been mistaken. He only had honest men in his outfit.

Mister Ab was so confident that he lifted the canvas flap of the supply wagon and invited the sheriff to take a look inside. But there, to our great dismay, lay the stolen fence railings! Mister Ab looked around for Butch, but he was nowhere to be found. Mister Ab paid the hefty fine for him—$2 a rail for thirty rails.

After the sheriff left, Butch mysteriously reappeared. Mister Ab let him have it. Then Butch repaid him. He handed Mister Ab three newly minted $20 gold pieces. He seemed to have a lot of them jingling in his vest pocket. Just how did he make that kind of money running cattle? A trail hand only makes $30 a month! And, if he has that much money, why was he so desperate to sign on with this outfit? Interesting how he hid from that sheriff. Just what is he running from exactly?

Saturday, June 15, 1878
Arrive Little Wichita River, Texas

Would you believe it? We've been trailing for a month and a half and we're still in Texas. I knew Texas was big, but I had no idea it had this much elbow room! This northern part we're in now is Big Sky Country. In every direction, I can see fifty miles away, no, make that one hundred. Pure wide open spaces. Those crazy camels would thrive out here. It's miles between water holes. The cattle get so thirsty their tongues just hang from their mouths.

As far as the eye can see, there's nothing but prairie dogs, sand, canyons, cactus, and rolling desert floor. Occasionally we'll pass some antelope, elk, or buffalo, but they're too wild to get close to. And you can forget about soothing Gulf breezes or restful shady groves out here. This part of Texas is hot, dry, and treeless (except near the occasional river or creek) with plenty of sun, sun, sun. The burning sand just crawls with rattlesnakes. Just walking around camp, I have to carry a stick for protection against snakes in my path.

Riding in the morning is tolerable. But, by early afternoon, it's a blazing oven! That's when the sun's right in our eyes. And, because of my "redheaded curse," I sunburn easily. You should see my wretched nose! Oh, how it stung at first. It sunburned so badly that it broke out in millions of tiny, red bubble blisters. Dovey put prickly pear gel on it. Now it's peeling. I've lost count of all the new freckles on my face. My lips are chapped and cracking. Mama will be furious! So, to keep from my ruining my skin even further, I now start the day as the cowboys do—standing behind the chuck wagon, dipping tar from the bucket that hangs there. Cookie keeps the black oil for greasing the wheel axles.

We slather the tar on our noses, cheeks, and lips. It smells awful but at least now I can talk without my lips bleeding.

I can't stand Butch Craven. He is pure evil. In this terrible drought, he rides his horses until they're hot, fussed, and in a lather. It makes Chico mad to see our horses so cruelly treated. Butch has a bad temper and cusses a lot—even in front of Dovey and me. He wears his black hat really low over his eyes. He looks like a badman. I wish Mister Ab would fire him. That's not going to happen, though. I overheard Chico tell Joe that we need all the cowboys we have to make it through Indian Territory. We'll be there in less than two weeks. Must be a pretty dangerous place, Indian Territory.

Since there's no timber out here, we're using buffalo chips (dung) for fuel. At first, I was disgusted at the idea of picking up something that came out the back end of a furry animal. But do you know what? When those chips burn, they don't smell at all. Also, their smudgy smoke wards off mosquitoes! Knowing that, Dovey and I happily load the wheelbarrow with buffalo chips! We call them "meadow muffins," which sounds more dignified. Now, if we could just come up with something to get rid of these giant stinging horseflies!

It's a good thing Butch brought a bandanna. Mister Ab gave him drag duty—riding at the back of the herd. Mister Ab makes all the troublemakers eat the dust of the trail. I hope Butch stays there the rest of the trip. He's creepy.

Monday, June 17, 1878
Arrive Wichita Falls, Texas

Wichita Falls is not much of a town. It's more of a trading post for buffalo hunters. This afternoon, thirteen different teams of buffalo hunters lined up to sell their skins and meat to a trader named Tom Buntin. One team of four Englishmen introduced themselves to us. They told us how, for three months, they have been living in tepees on the Brazos River and hunting buffalo. Some time back, they ran out of flour and coffee. They have gone the last three days without bread. Could they buy some flour from us? they wanted to know. Two were hunters; the other two were cooks and skinners. They were driving two light wagons pulled by horses.

At first, these foreigners fascinated me. The hunters had fancy waxed mustaches and eye monocles and said things like, "Jolly good!" and "Righto, old chap!" But when they began to talk about their hunt, I went from charmed to disgusted. They did not kill buffalo to make a living. They killed just for the sport of it. These men had come clear across the ocean just to hunt down our native animals for thrills and a little pocket change.

"On my first day out," bragged the big, beefy one who calls himself Charlie, "I picked off sixty-three buffs before I'd even had my morning tea! Once I killed their lead bull, the rest were putty in my hands."

The other hunter was just as arrogant. He said that buffaloes were "stupid beasts" because they are so easy to kill. "When they're grazing, I get downwind of them where they can't smell me," he said, chuckling, "then I take my six pounder and blow the whole lot of them to bits." He pretended to be shooting. "Kaboom!"

Then one of the skinners motioned for me to follow him to the wagon. It was stacked with dried buffalo hides eight feet high.

"Quite a haul, eh, matey?" he said, holding up one of the bull hides proudly. He showed me that it had no knife-gashes. "I bet I get top dollar for this one," he boasted. "Buntin sometimes pays $2 for a clean bull hide!" I can't imagine his buff hides turned into winter lap robes for northern buggy riders. They were surely thick enough but plenty scabby, too.

I guess I'm not such a great judge of character. When I first met the hunters, I thought they were two proper English gentlemen. But they turned out to be nothing but two bloodthirsty savages in clever disguise.

Thursday, June 20, 1878
At Buffalo Head Creek, Texas

We knew that something terrible was happening to the buffalo. Since leaving Decatur, we had heard an occasional boom of a buffalo rifle. But the more we traveled northwest, the more gunshots we heard. The gunshots have become continual cracks in the quiet of the prairie. We knew all along that slaughter awaited us ahead on the trail. We were unprepared, though, for the horror we faced.

It had been one of those waterless drives and our cattle were dying of thirst. We headed for Buffalo Head Creek. We prayed it wasn't dry. A few miles from the creek, it hit us—the most sickening stench I've ever smelled—that of rotting meat. I gagged and pulled my bandanna up over my mouth. Swarms of horseflies attacked us, our cattle, and our horses. The cattle moaned and swished their tails against the cactus to beat off the stinging flies. Their tails became mangled and bloody.

And then we saw it. Buffalo carcasses littered the prairie. The hunters had taken the hides and left the meat. Buzzards were busily ripping the meat from the bone. Orphaned calves stood over their dead mothers and bawled their heads off. Their sad cries stabbed my heart like a dagger.

Somehow Jeb knew what I was feeling. He mounted his horse and roped one of the orphaned buffalo heifers. He handed her over to Joe, who put her in the supply wagon with the Longhorn calves born on the trail. Next Jeb picked out an orphan buffalo bull calf and snared a loop on him. He gave Jeb a harder time than the heifer. That rascal ran under Jeb's horse, causing him to pitch all over the place. Jeb jumped off and hazed the bull calf over to the supply wagon, getting butted all the way. It was the only time I laughed all day. Jeb never said a word to me, but I knew this pair of buffalo calves was for me.

Joe One-Wing did something sneaky. He slipped the loose sacks belonging to Mrs. Bubbies' Longhorn calves over the two buff calves. He wants the scent of the Longhorn babies to rub off on the buffs. Hopefully, Mrs. Bubbies will mistake the buffs for her own, adopt them, and nurse them. I said a prayer to Jesus she would accept them.

After watering the herd, we camped down the road a piece where the air was fresher. For supper, Cookie fried up some buffalo meat. I had no stomach for it. I quietly nibbled a crust of bread. Will noticed.

"Hey, Hallie Lou," he yelled, gnawing on a stringy chunk of buffalo, "come on! Just take one itty bitty bite! You'll like it! It's not as good as our cattle but it's still good grub!" He dangled the meat in front of my face. "Open wide," he said. Everyone laughed.

Was this his idea of cheering me up? I know he was teasing but how rude! How little he knows me! Did it escape his attention how upset that slaughter made me? Out of the corner of my eye, I saw that Jeb didn't touch a scrap of buffalo meat either. He, too, made do with bread.

Before I went to bed, I checked on the buffs. Since the bull calf is so shaggy, I'll call him Samson. I guess that automatically makes the heifer Delilah.

Sunday, June 23, 1878
At Pease River, Texas

Morning

Yesterday, while crossing this dried-up river, ten steers bogged in the quicksand. The boys dug them out. We threw the herd on the prairie and camped for the night. We're all so thirsty. The water barrels are almost empty. Our throats are parched. Several steers have dropped dead in their tracks from thirst. Two days ago, the cattle smelled water and raced to drink from some bubbling springs, clear as crystal. But it was gyp water. Some drank the bad water and got poisoned. Joe and Chico wanted to dose the sick cattle with whiskey, but the whiskey bottle's missing from the chuckbox. The cattle are so dry, Mister Ab is worried about stampede. Just an hour ago, a few of the boys galloped ahead to scout for water holes. Without water, the herd won't be alive another day.

Dovey has fever. I hope she doesn't have the ague. The best cure for that is quinine, and I don't have any. Instead I gave her boneset to drop her temperature. Poor Dovey. It's a hundred in the shade and here she is, burning up with fever. I must save her.

Later

The boys found some waterholes up ahead a few miles by Salt Creek. They were clogged with dirt and sand. To get down to the water, the boys had to stand in the oozing mud and clean the holes out with shovels. When Jeb returned to show us the way there, he was limping. He must have fallen while digging and sprained his ankle. It took a lot of talking on my part, but I finally convinced him to let me bandage it. He sure is noble about pain. His ankle is terribly swollen, but he has not complained once that it hurts.

When we got to the water holes, I plastered some cool mud on Dovey's chest. Her fever makes her imagine things. She screams because she sees spiders walking around on me. There aren't any spiders.

You should have seen those cattle lap up that dirty water from those holes! Mrs. Bubbies led her calves to drink—all four of them. Does she not notice that the two new ones, Samson and Delilah, don't look a thing like her?

Monday, June 24, 1878
North of Salt Creek, Texas

Cookie thought some beef broth might give Dovey some strength. So, last night, he killed a fat yearling. He tied a rope to the front bow of the wagon and the other to a small tree. He hung the beef on the rope. He'll butcher the calf in the morning.

As usual, we were sleeping by the wagons when Will, Bud, and Ed rode into camp at midnight. They had been minding the cattle. When they went to wake the cowboys for the next shift, they discovered a panther was in our camp. He was standing on his hind feet eating the beef off the rope, just a stone's throw from where we were sleeping. When the panther saw the men, he let out the most horrifying scream I have ever heard in all my life. It made the hair on the back of my neck stand up. I sat straight up in bed and thought, "What's that?" It sounded just like a woman crying. Then I heard a gunshot. The panther had lunged, and Will had shot him dead.

Wednesday, June 26, 1878
At Doan's Store, Texas, just south of Doan's
  Crossing, the ford of the Red River

Morning

What a blessing to find a supply store out in the middle of nowhere! And one that carries quinine, too. I bought every bottle on the shelf, all ten of them, raced back to camp, and fed Dovey three heaping tablespoonfuls. If her fever doesn't break soon, I'll pour all ten bottles down her throat until it does! She's sicker than a dog. When an attack comes on, she calls out, *"Mamá! Mamá!"* It scares the cows and makes them moo. One minute, she's freezing cold and shivering. The next minute, she's burning up and sweating. If we were back at the Rockin' W, Gabby would know what to do. Cookie's mother died of the ague. Oh, Lord, please don't let Dovey die! I love her so—

Here at Doan's Store, nobody seems to care that I'm dressed like a man. Probably because there are so many rough characters in these parts. Every man carries a pistol and a rifle. When we first rolled into town, our wagons almost crushed three raggedy children drawing with sticks in the dirt road. Neither a mother nor a big sister watched over them. They must be cutting teeth. They were chewing on shotgun shells.

Thirty or forty Indians leaned against hitching posts. They carried dressed deer hides to trade. When two Texas Rangers rode up and tied up their horses, every one of the Indians scattered. The lawmen stationed themselves outside Doan's Store. As customers came out, they questioned them. The Rangers are hot on the trail of the train robber, Sam Bass. The postmaster reported that he saw Mr. Bass pass through Doan's Crossing only three days ago, disguised as a farmer.

This morning at breakfast, the cowboys were almost giggly about going into town. They slicked back their hair and combed their mustaches. I later found out what the fuss was all about. Just recently, two young girls who are cousins moved in with the Doan family. That makes a total of four females living at Doan's Crossing—Mrs. Doan, her daughter, and, now, the two cousins. The cousins make buckskin gloves for five dollars a pair. To get a fit, a man must have his hands measured. To have his hands measured by the hands of a lovely young woman is heaven on earth to a cowboy. This morning, after breakfast, Mister Ab gave the boys their pay and they were off to town, lickety-split.

Afternoon

After lunch, Cookie was feeding Dovey broth, so I felt comfortable leaving camp and returning to Doan's Store. I wanted to buy some sugar cubes for Rosie. She's been such a faithful pony. The outfit was already in town except for Bud, Butch, and John R. They were watching the herd. Originally, Will had been scheduled for day duty. However, when Butch found out that Will wanted to go into town, he offered to take his duty. How unlike Butch to sacrifice a good time! Now why wouldn't he want to go into town like the rest of the boys?

When I got to the store, I was surprised to find Jeb there. He was talking with a shop girl working behind the counter. She was by far the most gorgeous girl I have ever seen in my entire life. Her silky blond hair was swept up in a bun and pinned with a tortoise shell tucking comb. Her skin was creamy white. Her cheeks gave off a pink glow and her mouth was like a red, red rose. She must be one of the cousins.

When Jeb saw me, he put his elbows on the counter and leaned closer to her. He lowered his voice to a whisper. Was Jeb just like the other boys, hankering for a touch of soft female flesh?

I pretended to shop. I wandered over to the glass display case and looked in. I saw my reflection. . . . Yikes! My hair was as tangled as a bird's nest! My face was as brown as old boot leather! No wonder Jeb looks at her and not at me! The display case contained wonderful treats: peppermint sticks and chewing gum, rose water, and an assortment of tucking combs. One of the combs was similar to the one in the pretty girl's hair but slightly different. It was made of mother-of-pearl. I wanted that comb. I needed all the help I could get on my appearance!

I dashed out front to get some coins from my saddlebag. I was gone three minutes, at most. Yet, when I returned, the combs were gone and so was Jeb! I was so flustered that I left the store empty-handed. Poor Rosie, old girl. I was clear back to camp before I realized I had forgotten to get her sugar!

Late Evening

We are not alone on this trail. I cannot begin to guess how many cattle are being walked this spring from South Texas to Dodge up this one trail. 50,000? 500,000? Often, in our march, we've been driven off land by ferocious dogs or have run into fences. Always, though, Mister Ab redirected our outfit so the cattle got enough grass to live upon. The Indian Territory is the cowpuncher's paradise. It's one grand expanse of free grass.

While we were filling our water barrels and canteens at the river today, several horsemen rode up. Their leader was a cattle inspector. He told Mister Ab to string the cattle out into a line to be sure they all belonged to us. We must have accidentally picked up a few strays on the way because they found five little unbranded dogies. They took them away. Mister Ab then paid the man seventy-five dollars for examining the herd. They gave us a clean bill of health. We could cross the Red River and enter Indian Territory.

Often, the Red River is swift, treacherous, and full of swirling quicksand. But today, it is low and easily forded. We'll cross it in the morning.

We can see Indian signal fires burning on the other side of the river. Tomorrow we'll be over there—in the Indian Territory. I wonder what the Indians are saying to each other with those strange fires. Are they warning each other we are coming? Or, more likely, are they planning an attack?

Thursday, June 27, 1878
Still south of the Red River in Texas

Morning

Something terrible happened to me last night. Butch Craven broke into my tent. Fortunately, I heard him as he tripped over the lantern by the tent flap. I woke up before he could hurt me. I sat up straight in bed and pulled the covers over my nightgown. I could smell him across the room. He reeked of whiskey and sweat. He was stinking drunk.

He grinned at me in a way that made my skin crawl. "Don't be afraid, little lady," he purred, wickedly. "All I want is a little sugar." He stumbled toward me. He was going to kiss me! Then, suddenly, he lost his balance and fell flat across my chest.

I was quick. I reached under my pillow and grabbed my pistol. I shoved it between his ribs. "Get up!" I growled. "Get out of here this minute or I'll shoot!" I almost suffocated under his weight.

He was mad, but he did what I said because I was the one holding the gun. As he was leaving, he looked back at me. "You'd better watch out, Miss Priss," he said, "I'll get even with you yet."

This is torture. I can't tell anybody what happened, not even Dovey. She'd tell Cookie and he'd tell Mister Ab. Mister Ab would fire Butch on the spot. He'd feel duty-bound to defend my honor. He'd be none too happy that Butch was drinking either, especially drinking the whiskey that he stole from our medicine chest. But Mister Ab can't fire Butch, even if he is a low-down skunk. We need every hand we've got to guard our cattle and horses in Indian Territory. We can't do without one man. I can't do that to the boys. They've been rubbing their six-shooters bright since we reached the Red River. They're nervous and on guard. They know that, once we cross this river, we leave civilization—and the law—behind.

So, I'll put on an act. On the outside, I'll be cool. On the inside, however, I'll be tied up in knots.

On the North Fork of the Red River, Indian Territory

Evening

God has answered my prayer. Today, I kept my lip buttoned and uttered not a word about Butch to a soul. Instead, I prayed unceasingly for God to deliver me. And he has. Here it is, my first night to camp in the Indian Territory, and I'm not one bit afraid. God sent me an earth angel—Dooley. Out of the blue, Jeb decided to station Dooley outside my tent every night while we're in the Territory. Jeb says it's because the men can't guard me and the cattle and the horses all at the same time. Whew, what a relief! If Dooley wasn't here, I could never fall to sleep. I would have worried about what would get me first—the Indians, outlaws, cattle rustlers, wolves, or Butch Craven! But tonight I'll sleep like a baby.

After we crossed the river this morning, we saw a sign that said we were entering the Kiowa-Comanche Reservation. It said that the fee for grazing our cattle was "one wohaw," meaning one steer. The grass is excellent in this lush valley. Mister Ab says that, for the next five days, fresh lakes will border the trail.

At mid-morning, some Comanches rode up to collect their fee. They were very businesslike. Mister Ab picked out a high-grade steer, very fat, about a fifteen-hundred pounder, and gave it to them. Mister Ab made sure the steer was a fine one. If these warriors got angry, he told us later, they'd shoot arrows into the herd and cause a stampede. During the commotion, they'd cut out as many cattle as they wanted.

When Mister Ab handed over the steer, at least a dozen of the Indians raised their guns and shot it at once. In less than ten minutes, they had the beef skinned, cut up, and packed on their ponies. Then they were gone.

Friday, June 28, 1878
At North Fork of Red River, Indian Territory

Mid-afternoon

Dovey's better. I guess her body is finally saturated with quinine. It's a good thing, too. The quinine is used up. The medicine she took should hold her for about two to three weeks. Then I'll have to dose her all over again. Cookie is thrilled that she's eating solid food again. He gathered some turtle eggs from the riverbank and scrambled them for her. She gave us both a scare—but she's not out of the woods yet.

We're following this river north for several miles. Its banks are covered in wild plums. The trees are so loaded with luscious fruit that the branches drag the ground. At noon, we stopped and picked yellow, red, and blue plums.

While we were stopped, Joe One-Wing wandered off into some tall grass and flushed out some wild turkeys. One gobbler gave him a good chase, but Joe finally caught up with him. Tonight, we'll have a different supper menu—stewed wild turkey and plum pie. I'm eating dessert first. And, if there's any pie left over, I'll be really naughty and have another piece for breakfast!

Saturday, June 29, 1878
Leaving North Fork of Red River,
Indian Territory

Mid-morning

What a close call that was! It happened when we were packing up camp and getting ready to hit the trail. The cowboys were unmuffling the bells on Mrs. Bubbies and El Tuerto.

I was alone in camp. Joe was cleaning the breakfast dishes down at the river. Cookie had fed his six mules and had harnessed them to the chuck wagon. He and Dovey had taken the water barrels down to the river to fill. I was sitting on a camp stool under a shade tree writing my mother a letter.

I had just been writing her an unflattering description of the Indian Territory—flat, red, hot, dry, dusty, and very, very windy. I told her about how last night's special supper was almost spoiled because this blasted wind blew ashes, sand, and dirt into the stewed turkey. Every bite was gritty. I was engrossed in writing my letter when I heard the mules shuffling about. I looked up to find dozens of Indians around the chuck wagon. Some of them were climbing up over the wheels, while others were trying to lift the wagon sheet to look inside. My heart started skipping beats. Just then I heard Cookie whistling as he came up the bluff.

Cookie must have sensed danger. He put down his water barrel and looked around. He saw what was happening. Immediately, he walked to our campsite, bent down, and grabbed his six-foot mule whip. It was lying on the ground between him and the wagon.

Cookie began to whirl that lash around his head. It popped like pistol shots. The Indians stood as if made of stone. To keep them still, Cookie walked toward the wagon, yelling, "Back, back!" all the while slapping right and left at the Indians, bucks and squaws alike, with his whip.

The old squaws began crying: "Mush away! Mush away!" They were begging for bread.

Still popping his whip as he pushed his hands under the wagon sheet, Cookie pulled out a fifty-pound can filled with cooked beans, potatoes, onions, dried beef, and stale bread. He had been saving it up for just such an emergency! The Indians were thrilled and didn't seem to want to make any further trouble. But Cookie was taking no chances. He drove them from camp with his popping whip. As they passed out of sight, I saw the bucks fighting among themselves over the feast.

I never knew Cookie had such courage. He's always been such a mild-mannered, if cranky, fellow. My hero!

Sunday, June 30, 1878
Halfway between North Fork and Salt Fork
of the Red River, Indian Territory

Midday

It's not normal for us to be camped in the heat of the day miles away from a creek or a river. But it's not a normal day. The whole face of the earth is covered with a herd of wild animals, all moving in the same direction south. We had to stop our herd to let them pass. Droves of buffalo, mustangs, elk, deer, antelope, wolves, and some wild cattle are all mixed together. Several hours have already passed and we have yet to see the end of this migration. Mister Ab says there are more animals in this herd than he has ever seen of any living thing. The boys rode on ahead to keep the buffalo from stampeding our herd.

I think we're all a little homesick and weary of the trail.

Things I miss: my feather bed, bubble baths, Gabby's lemonade, reading a book up high in my chinaberry tree where no one can see me, the Gulf breeze, afternoon naps, bedtime prayers with Mama, playing checkers with Gussie, trying to pet China Doll, hugging Papa, teasing Ray, and safety from Indians and wolves and Butch Craven.

Things I don't miss: Miss Strickland!

Monday, July 1, 1878
In foothills of the Wichita Mountains,
on north bank of the North Fork of the
Red River, Indian Territory

In my fourteen years, I have never known a summer this hot. Today, the wind simply refused to blow. The sun beat down on us as we wearily rode across this flat and treeless prairie. I almost fainted in the saddle. It's a good thing I laid in a large supply of bandannas in Fort Worth. Today, I used five of them to mop my forehead. We sure could use some rain to cool things off and wet things down. The herd is surrounded by a cloud of dust that burns our eyes and chokes us.

That Butch Craven is a bad man! While we were stopped for lunch, I found him snooping around my buggy. He said he was admiring its "fine craftsmanship." I don't believe that for a minute. Then, about mid-afternoon, when I was riding up front of the herd, he rode up alongside me wearing nothing but his undershirt and drawers! How vulgar! I was just as hot as he was but you didn't see me stripping off my clothes and riding around in my corset and pantaloons! He was trying to shock me. I yanked back the reins on Rosie. I waited until the herd passed, choosing to lag behind with the drags, the yearlings, Chico and the horses, and my buggy.

Jeb must have been watching me, because a few minutes later, he trotted up alongside me. He was upset.

"Miss Hallie," he said, "I forbid you to ride drag. Come at once to the front." With that said, he turned his horse and rode back to the front. No explanation. No please. No thank you. Just do it.

I tried to swallow but there was a lump in my throat. What could I have done to make him that mad? Would he judge me so harshly if he knew about Butch Craven? Tears welled up in my eyes.

Chico saw my misery. He was quick to explain. "Don't take it so hard, Miss Hallie," he said. "Jeb means well. Them Indians just make him nervous." He told me that females crossing the Territory were in great danger. Indians liked to kidnap women because they brought such high ransoms. Riding at the back made me "easy pickin's for Injuns," said Chico.

Was that really it? Was Jeb being protective? Did he just want to keep me in sight? Or, was he just bossing me around in the line of duty?

This evening, after we crossed the river, we found Quanah Parker and a Comanche friend waiting for us.

Will says that Quanah Parker had a Comanche father and a white mother. He is a great war chief and believes a man should have many wives! He was dressed just like a white man except that he wore his hair in two long, black braids. He had on a hat and pants with a six-shooter, cowboy style. His friend, though, wore a breechclout and hunting skirt and had a Winchester tied to his saddle.

Quanah's friend said, "Me heap hungry." He made it quite plain that he wanted something to eat by motioning with his finger toward his mouth. Quanah was friendly, but I didn't trust his friend. They were satisfied with the yearling Mister Ab gave them and went on their way.

I'm in my tent right now, writing by lamplight. The boys are by the fire, swapping stories. I don't usually pay much attention because they mostly talk about horses and cattle. But tonight's conversation is far juicier. They're talking about that pretty blonde who works back at Doan's Store. Her name is Vanessa. I wonder if Jeb did buy her those tucking combs—

Tuesday, July 2, 1878
At Crooked Creek, Indian Territory

This morning we passed through a gap in the Wichita Mountains. They're less mountains than giant boulders. They're made of solid rock—granite, says Mister Ab. When the mountains are in shadow, they are orangey-brown and naked. But when the sun shines on them, they sparkle like they're studded with diamonds.

Cookie misses the firewood of the cross timbers, but our cattle are thriving on this prairie grass. Every evening, Dovey and I pull grass and twist it into coils for our breakfast fire. We are grateful, though, when we find buffalo chips to use for fuel instead. It's less smoky when it burns.

At lunch, Butch Craven started a prairie fire. He was showing off, shooting matches for sport. Within seconds, the grass all around us was in a blaze. It spread so quickly that the men could not stop it. They beat out the flanks of the fire so that it did not spread into our camp. The fire blazed higher than a house and went straight ahead for fifty miles or more. Birds and animals fled before the flames. The cattle stampeded and it was hours before we had them all rounded up again. Butch Craven is so reckless. I fear what he will do next.

Wednesday, July 3, 1878
At Elk Creek, Indian Territory

The grass is growing sparser. The many herds ahead of us on the trail have eaten the range off. We trailed the herd all day without stopping once to graze. When we got to this creek, the cattle and horses were starved. After drinking their fill, the cattle stood on their hind feet like dogs to eat moss out of the trees. Some horses ate the bark off chinaberry trees. If only it would rain. The earth is parched with thirst.

Investigators came today to find out who set yesterday's fire. They interviewed Butch Craven. I guess they were satisfied with what he told them because they rode off without a word.

We get the feeling we're being watched. We haven't seen any Indians in several days but we know they're out there. We see their moccasin tracks at the fords on all the streams. This morning, we found a newly dug grave on the east side of the trail. Its tombstone read, "killed by Indians." We watch our horses like hawks, fearing a raid. To lose our saddle ponies would spell our doom.

I'm having trouble sleeping tonight because the wolves are howling close to camp. They are snapping and snarling like they're fighting over a carcass. I can't stop thinking of a story Joe One-Wing told of how a Comanche can imitate a wild beast to signal another Comanche to attack. Were those wolves out there or Comanches? I don't know which would be worse. Either way, I have both my trusty rifle and my pistol by my side. And I'm not afraid to use them, either.

Thursday, July 4, 1878
At Cash Creek, Indian Territory

American Independence Day

They say trouble comes in threes. If it does, we've certainly paid our dues.

Last night, while I was sleeping, Chico was standing guard over the horses. He struck a match to light his cigarette. As he did so, somebody shot at him three times in a row. The boys at camp grabbed their guns and returned the fire. The Indians were trying to scare us away from our horses so they could get them. Thank the Lord, it didn't work. It would be a nightmare to be stuck out here without a horse.

This afternoon, a man passed us on the trail. His name was Arnett. He was also riding north to Dodge. He warned us to look out for Indians. We thanked him and he rode on ahead. This evening, when we made camp, we found his bloody clothes by the creek.

The third bad thing happened to Will. This morning, before daylight, he had loped out to a little hill to see if he could spy any Indians. His horse stumbled and fell, throwing him and breaking his left collarbone. It was all he could do to climb back up on that horse and ride to camp. I rolled up a shirt tightly and tied it under his arm. I then bound his arm to his body. He smiled and gave me a little peck on the cheek. I know I turned red! Out of the corner of my eye, I saw Jeb watching with a frown. The boys then lifted Will up and put him in the supply wagon. Joe fixed him a little bed across the boxes. He'll be laid up at least a week nursing that broken collarbone.

Three calamities in less than twenty-four hours didn't make for a very happy Fourth of July celebration. But we gave it our best try. We didn't want to spoil the special dinner Cookie had prepared. We had a fine stew that we sopped up with biscuits as golden-topped, light and tasty as I've ever had. For dessert, we had a Brown Betty of dried apples and a sauce. The boys serenaded us with marching band music. Our merry faces masked our troubled hearts. What further danger lies ahead?

Saturday, July 6, 1878
At the Washita River, Indian Territory

Late afternoon

We were glad to finally reach the Washita last night. This is our last watering hole before we make the long, waterless drive to the Canadian River. That dry stretch will be thirty miles long. We've been moving at twelve miles a day. We'll have to really push the cattle to go faster so that we can reach the Canadian before they die of thirst. The grass is so sparse between watering holes now that our little Southern steers are beginning to look like racehorses. It still hasn't rained. Today, we are resting, to let the herd drink and graze on this tall grass.

This morning, forty Comanches appeared in camp. Every one of them held a parasol. Mister Ab asked them where they had been. One of them spoke up, in fairly good English. He said they had been up north at the Arkansas River, making a treaty with another tribe. I think they must have stolen those parasols.

One of the other bucks asked for "terback." Mister Ab handed him a plug of tobacco. He gave two of his friends each a chew, took one himself, and stuck the rest in his pocket. I thought we were going to have a scene when Mister Ab asked the buck for his plug back. But the Indian didn't get mad. Cookie gave the man who spoke English a bag of sugar and they rode off into the west.

Sunday, July 7, 1878
13 miles north of the Washita River,
Indian Territory

Do I detect a little jealousy on Jeb's part? This morning, I rode alongside the supply wagon, driven by Joe One-Wing. I took it upon myself to scout out the road ahead and direct Joe to the parts of the trail that were less rutted. With every bump of the road, poor Will gets a fresh jab of pain. I just thought that the less jostling about, the better he'd feel and the quicker he'd mend. I had been on the job only a half hour when Bud appeared. He'd received orders to relieve me, he said. Jeb sent him. If Jeb is jealous of Will and me, then it serves him right. How does he think I felt back at Doan's Store with him drooling over Vanessa?

What a terrible dry spell. There is so little growing here that you could see a jackrabbit a mile away. To stake our horses without trees, we had to bury their ropes in the sand. We made a dry camp tonight. The cattle are bawling for water.

Monday, July 8, 1878
Five miles south of the Canadian River
Indian Territory

I played with the cutest little animals today. They're called prairie dogs, but they're not dogs at all. They just bark like them. They're more like squirrels. They have brown fur and tails tipped in black. They're nervous little creatures. Standing on their hind legs, they guard the entrance to their underground homes. If they sense danger, they bark. That sends an alarm signal for everyone in Dog Town to scurry down their holes and hide. Mister Ab says their homes are connected by an underground network of tunnels. What's so amazing is that the same prairie dog might duck down one hole and pop up in a completely different one several feet away. A prairie dog reminds me of a jack-in-the-box.

Some of the boys thought they'd use the prairie dogs for target practice, even Will, who winced with pain every time he shot his rifle. The prairie dogs were too quick and outwitted them every time. I was glad. I was also disgusted with Will. Imagine him picking on such innocent little creatures for sport. No more Florence Nightingale for me! Let Joe One-Wing change his bandage tomorrow.

I can't wait to reach the Canadian tomorrow. Mister Ab says it's a wide river with plenty of water for the cattle. That's good because they're close to dying of thirst.

Tuesday, July 9, 1878
On the north bank of the Canadian River
Indian Territory

We were only a mile out of camp this morning before a wheel axle broke on the chuck wagon. It did not take very long to fix it, only a few hours, but when we did

108

start, it was close to noon and the sun was high. The horses seemed harder than usual to drive and to keep on the trail. The cattle were irritable. They were restless and thirsty.

About five o'clock, we saw a long line of straggling trees directly ahead of us. They seemed to be burning at the ground. Clouds of what we thought were smoke rose from their trunks. When we got closer, we saw that it was not smoke; it was drifting sand driven by the wind. This Canadian River was not the wide but shallow river that Mister Ab remembered. That must have been during the rainy season. This Canadian was a dry zone of drifting sands. Our hearts sank and we feared the worst. Was there no water?

Then we heard Jeb shout, "Water!" God had not forsaken us. One small, life-giving stream flowed in a narrow channel through the dry creek bed. There was more than enough water to go around. The banks were long lines of sand dunes piled about thickets of wild plum bushes. Between the river and the hills beyond was a rich, green valley. We grazed our herd for several hours before bedding them down for the night.

Thursday, July 11, 1878
At junction of Powwow Creek and the
Canadian River, Indian Territory

Will tried to ride horseback this morning. Chico saddled up his horse. He started out riding along behind the herd. But as soon as his horse struck a trot, the pain became unbearable. He had to return to the wagon.

We saw some smoke signals northeast of us. Jeb rode out to investigate. He was gone for hours. When he arrived back in camp, he was galloping and out of breath. He had spotted a Kiowa camp just north of here. About thirty tepees were set up in a small grove. Mister Ab thinks they've gathered for their annual Sun Dance. It lasts ten days. Afterwards, the warriors go on raids. Mister Ab says we'll move out first thing in the morning. Kiowas are dangerous.

Friday, July 12, 1878
At Powwow Creek, Indian Territory

Noon

At sunrise, about two hundred Kiowa bucks, squaws, and children showed up at our camp. The bucks had on war paint. They were led by two men, Chief Bacon Rind and Sundown, a pock-marked half-breed.

Of all the men there, only Sundown dismounted. The other Indian bucks stayed on horseback. The squaws sat down together by a clump of bushes. Some had papooses on their backs. The papooses picked around in their mother's hair looking for lice. Then they ate them.

Sundance spoke some English. He said, "Me speak to heap big boss." Mister Ab stepped forward. Sundance demanded food and meat.

Mister Ab spread a tarp on the ground between him and Sundown. From the chuck wagon, he brought forth a small amount of flour, sugar, coffee, bacon, prunes, dried apples, beans, and some canned peaches. He placed it in full view so the Kiowas could see what he was offering them to depart in peace. Henry brought a nice, fat cow forward to show them the meat.

111

But Sundown was in an ugly mood. He became furious. "Cow no good for Indians—good for white man—Indians want big steer!"

"No deal," Mister Ab said, firmly. "I promised you meat. A cow is meat."

Sundance crossed his arms over his chest and looked around. Then he spied our lead steer, El Tuerto, standing with Chico and the horses by the supply wagon. "Me want that steer!" he said, pointing at El Tuerto.

Mister Ab shook his head. "It's the cow or nothing," said Mister Ab, crossing his arms over his chest, turning, and walking away. He would have fought the whole Indian Nation to keep his trained bell steer. Without El Tuerto in the lead, he knew the herd would be lost.

Some of the Indians seemed satisfied and were willing to accept the offer, but others wanted more. Sundance got them all excited. Old Chief Bacon Rind got down off his horse. He sat on the ground and lit his pipe. Then some really big bucks got down off their horses. They began gathering stones and building a mound in front of Chief Bacon Rind. They were building a fire.

Some of our boys got nervous. They knew that the Indians were getting ready to do a war dance.

Will tried to talk Mister Ab into giving up El Tuerto. "Pardon me, sir, but he's only a steer!" he said. "There are hundreds more just like him!"

But to Mister Ab, El Tuerto was not "only a steer." There was no other steer like him. El Tuerto was his buddy. He had led every one of Mister Ab's herds to Kansas for eleven straight years, in the fall and in the spring. Through dust and hail and rain and snow and drought and famine, El Tuerto had stuck by him. Now it was Mister Ab's turn to stick by El Tuerto.

Meanwhile, the Indians continued to prepare the fire. Once they'd stacked the stones in a mound, the bucks gathered sticks, leaves, and brush and placed them on top. Then Chief Bacon Rind lit the rubbish with his flint. The flames leapt into the air. The bucks danced around, chanting and beating their tom-toms. With their war dance, they hoped to frighten Mister Ab into giving up El Tuerto.

Then Jeb appeared on the scene leading the former outlaw and now lead bull, Ole Red, by a rope. "Take red bull," he said to Sundance. Jeb wasn't about to stand idly by and watch Mister Ab forced to sacrifice the one animal he loved most in the whole wide world. He offered a sacrifice instead—the bull he'd been grooming to lead a herd.

But Sundance was disagreeable—and greedy. He refused to accept Ole Red. He wanted El Tuerto.

By now, Mister Ab had had enough of this Indian. He decided to call his bluff. He told Cookie and Joe to put all the stuff he'd offered the Indians back in the chuck wagon. He yelled for Jeb and the boys to straddle their horses and round up the herd. "We're movin' out!" he shouted.

Sundance had lost—and he knew it. "Indians take Big Red Bull," said Sundance, hurriedly picking up the rope and walking toward his horse. Quickly, the squaws began gathering the food from the tarp and loading it onto their horses.

Then, just as everything seemed to be getting better, everything went haywire. A gunshot rang out. Then another and another and another. The next thing we knew, Mister Ab was lying on the ground with a bullet hole in his chest.

The Kiowas must have thought some of their Indian enemies were attacking them. They rode off like lightning, leaving both the food and Ole Red behind.

This is what happened. While Mister Ab was parleying with Sundance, a few of the bucks had walked over to Butch. One of them had asked him for "terback," or tobacco. Butch thought he'd play a joke on him. He got the tar bucket from the back of the chuckwagon and handed it to the Indian. The Indian was not amused to receive a tar bucket instead of "terback." A fight broke out and some guns went off. One of the bullets strayed and shot our beloved Mister Ab.

He is still alive, but barely. He's lost a lot of blood and has a bullet lodged in his chest. We have to get him to a doctor fast.

Curse the day Butch Craven was born! He's the devil himself!

At Turkey Creek, Indian Territory

Evening

We rode the last five miles in dead silence. We are just devastated by what happened this morning. What will we do without our leader? Mister Ab is still with us, but he's fading fast. He's lying on a stretcher being pulled behind Chico's horse. He goes in and out of consciousness.

We're detouring to Fort Supply. That trip will take about four days. Dear Jesus, I pray, help Mister Ab hang on until we reach a doctor.

El Tuerto moaned the whole way here. He knows why Mister Ab is not riding the point with him. He saw him get shot. He's so blue he can barely put one hoof in front of the other. Ole Red is keeping the herd moving. He's going to make a great bell bull some day.

Saturday, July 13, 1878
Turkey Creek, Indian Territory

Morning

All of us but Butch were gathered around when Mister Ab quit breathing last night. Since sundown, he had been unconscious and had not spoken.

So we were startled when, a little before midnight, he opened his eyes and cried out frantically, "Jeb! Jeb!"

"I'm right here, sir," said Jeb, rushing to his side.

Mister Ab seemed anxious to tell him something. "Bolivar," he whispered, "Bolivar . . . "

Jeb leaned forward to listen. "Yes, I'm here," he replied.

"You've got it, . . . Bolivar," whispered Mister Ab, straining to get out the words. "You've got . . . the gift . . . you're a real . . . cowboy . . . " The words drifted off into the stillness of the black night. For our fearless leader had closed his weary eyes and gone to his Maker.

Cookie, Mister Ab's oldest friend, straightened out his body. He pulled a sheet over it and put a quarter over each of his eyes to keep them shut. He lighted a candle to burn by the body and sat up with it all night until daybreak.

We would have liked to have buried Mister Ab in a pine coffin. But we couldn't wait until we ran into a carpenter. A body decomposes fast in the hot summer. We had to get his body into the ground right away.

Joe dug his grave with an ax. We buried him on the banks of a lonely creek among the wild roses. He was wrapped only in his bed blanket. John R. insisted that we bury him facing east. He explained, "Well, it's because when Jesus comes, He is going to come from the east. That way, when Mister Ab rises up to meet Him, he will be facing Him."

After we had mounded up the dirt, we piled stones on top to keep the wolves away. Cookie carved his tombstone. No one knew how old Mister Ab was. The tombstone said, "Ab Blocker, Texan, died July 13,

1878; he got the herds through in quick time & in fine shape."

Jeb sang, "Oh, bury me not on the lone prairie." Will played his banjo and Henry played his fife. The cattle lowed in the distance. I read from the Book of Common Prayer: "Dust thou art, and unto dust shalt thou return." We each picked up a handful of dirt and sprinkled it upon the grave. We wept and wept. We are so sad. How terribly we will miss you, dear Mister Ab—

Jesus, why did Mister Ab have to die? Why do you answer some of my prayers and not others?

Evening

I didn't realize it was my birthday until Cookie brought out a honey cake after supper. Everyone sang "Happy Birthday." It cheered me up some. I opened the present from my parents. It is a gorgeous gold locket with "H.L.W." carved on the front in fancy letters. The locket opens up. There's a space inside to put a photo or a lock of hair. When I'm feeling more like myself, I'll put something in it. But, while I'm sad, I'll just keep my locket where it's been so far—in its little box in the buggy pocket.

Will King can't stand it when everyone's not happy. "Let's dance!" he shouted. I refused, saying it was inappropriate on the day of our trail leader's death.

"Mister Ab was an old man!" he said. "He lived a long life. Let's get happy!"

If Will can snap his fingers and go from sad to happy, then he's not a very deep person. That reminds me of what that fortune teller in Fort Worth was saying. "Still waters run deep." Well, she certainly couldn't have seen Will King in my future. Will King is neither still nor deep!

Sunday, July 14, 1878
At Buzzard Creek, Indian Territory

I wonder where my new locket is? I went to go put it on today and it was gone, box and all. I know I put it in the buggy pocket last night —

It's raining!

Tuesday, July 16, 1878
At 25 Mile Creek, Indian Territory

This creek is bankfull. Trees are floating down it on big, foam-capped waves. Although it was rough, we went ahead and crossed to the other side. It could always rise even more overnight. Before I got across, I had to slip off Rosie's back and into the swift water. I held onto her tail as she swam us to the other side. Cookie unharnessed his mules and let them swim across. The boys attached ropes to the chuckwagon and floated it across.

Dovey's ill. I fear the worst. Her fever just keeps climbing. She needs quinine. When Jeb heard this, he mounted his horse and rode fifteen miles to Fort Supply for medicine. He made Will acting trail boss in his absence. Now it's raining harder. I hope Jeb doesn't try to ride back in this storm!

Wednesday, July 17, 1878
At 25 Mile Creek, Indian Territory

Evening

Jeb returned with the quinine. Thank the Lord! He was drenched and sneezing his head off. He also brought us a keg of pickles, because Cookie has been worried about us getting scurvy. (Now that he mentions it, I have noticed some bruises on my arm and my gums have been bleeding a little.)

After Jeb had gotten into some dry clothes, he shared the bad news: we've been quarantined. All Texas herds trailing into Kansas are being routed to a strip of country here in the Indian Territory called "No Man's Land." There we will have to wait until inspectors come to check our cattle. Kansas ranchers are worried that our Longhorns might carry Texas fever and spread it to their cattle.

Another delay. Maybe I'll develop some patience before this trip is over.

Saturday, July 20, 1878
No Name Creek in No Man's Land,
Indian Territory

For three days, we've waited for the inspectors and no one has come. Other herds are camped nearby. Our herd is getting restless. At least the grass is good here on the high plains.

Jeb is nervous about something. He can't be worried about Texas fever. He's always dusting the cattle for ticks.

Dovey's showing improvement.

Sunday, July 21, 1878
No Name Creek in No Man's Land,
Indian Territory

What a bizarre turn of events! All along, I believed we were waiting on cattle inspectors before we could resume our journey. Of course, that's what Jeb wanted us all to believe. If he had told us the truth, it would have spoiled his plan.

It was just after lunch today that we saw a group of horsemen approaching from the southeast. I assumed they were cattle inspectors, but they weren't. When they got closer, I could see their badges. They were Texas Rangers. They came to get Butch Craven. He's a train robber! He belongs to Sam Bass's gang!

Butch must have seen them coming. He took cover behind my buggy. He started taking potshots at the Rangers. That wasn't very smart, since there were so many of them and only one of him. The Rangers returned his fire. One of the bullets grazed Butch's left arm. He knew he was had. He threw his gun on the ground and put his hands in the air. They handcuffed and frisked him. And what do you suppose they found? My locket! Plus a pouch of newly minted, $20 gold pieces stolen from a Union Pacific passenger train he had robbed in Nebraska last fall. As they took him away, he hissed at me over his shoulder.

This is what happened: When Jeb was in Fort Supply, he went by the post office to mail my letter to Mama. He ran into those men who had ridden out to inspect the fire Butch had set. They told Jeb that they suspected that Butch was a member of the Sam Bass gang. One of the gang members had become an informant for the Rangers, they said. He had drawn them pictures of the gang. The fire inspectors showed Jeb these pictures. There in the stack was a likeness of Butch Craven, also known as "the Red Raider." He was called that because he has red hair. I was right! He was putting shoe black on his hair to cover up the red color!

The fire inspectors told Jeb to take his herd to No Man's Land and wait. They'd wire the Rangers to pick up Butch. The rest is history.

Wednesday we'll be in Kansas.

Tuesday, July 23, 1878
At Hog Creek, Indian Territory

Afternoon

Oh, my darling Jeb! He was been bitten by a rattlesnake! I am sick with worry. It's a miracle that giant rattler didn't break his leg. That snake must have been six feet long.

It all happened after lunch. We were camped on a creek in a shady oak grove. I had gone down into the desert with my wheelbarrow to gather buffalo chips. All of a sudden, Dooley appeared, breaking the silence. He ran, barking his head off, and began tearing at my trouser leg with his teeth. Something was terribly wrong. I dropped the wheelbarrow and raced after him.

I found Jeb a few hundred feet away, lying on the canyon floor. He had been bitten by a rattlesnake. Three feet away, the huge rattler was coiled, ready to strike him again. I pulled out my pistol and shot it.

I thought fast. With my pocket knife, I cut the left leg of his trousers and peeled it back. The wound was right above his boot. The two fang marks oozed venom. I quickly cut around the wound. I asked Jeb if he had any salt and he pointed to his leather pouch. I found some beef jerky. I chewed the salt out of it and spat out the meat. I then put my mouth on the open wound and sucked out the poison. I did this several times, each time spitting out the poison. Will and John R. must have heard my gunshot, because, at this point, they rode up. They loaded Jeb on a horse and carried him back to camp.

Once we got there, Cookie mixed up a poultice of turpentine and wet soda and plastered it on the wound. We've done everything humanly possible to save him. Now we can only wait—and pray.

At West Fork Creek, Indian Territory

Evening

Jeb's so pale. He's burning up with fever. His leg wound is black and blue and swollen. Cookie's seen a lot of snakebite before. He says this one looks bad. He swears that Jeb would be dead already, were it not for my heroic rescue.

I don't care about compliments. I care about Jeb. He just has to live. I pray every minute.

We cross the Cimarron River tomorrow. We hope to be in Kansas by noon. I should be excited but I'm not. All I can think about is Jeb.

Wednesday, July 24, 1878
At West Fork Creek, Indian Territory

Morning

Jeb's still confined to bed. I took it upon myself to ride two miles up the trail and scope out the Cimarron River ford. I had expected it to be a routine crossing.

With so little rain, I knew the Cimarron would not be swollen and easy to cross.

I was wrong. The river I found is far deadlier than a swollen one. This river is so low that it is full of salt. The salt crystals look like a field of snow upon a sandy riverbed. At least cattle can drink from a swollen river. If an animal drinks from this salty stream, it will die. Somehow, we must get the herd across that river without permitting a single animal to drink. And we must do it without Jeb or Mister Ab in the lead.

Thursday, July 25, 1878
At Five Mile Creek, Kansas

Noon

Yesterday, we made it across the salty river without any cattle stopping to drink. We stampeded them across. We whipped the herd with ropes and whooped and hollered to keep them moving. Ole Red and El Tuerto did a wonderful job without Mister Ab or Jeb working the point.

Our troubles began, though, after we had crossed. The thirsty herd kept trying to turn back. It was getting dark before we finally got them just a mile from the river. All night long, they tried to escape to the river to drink. Littered around our camp were dead cattle from other herds that had drunk the briny water. The smell of their rotting flesh reminded us to be on our guard. None of us slept a wink.

We hit the trail at sunrise, thirsty. Then, finally, about 10:00 A.M. today, we found this little freshwater creek. The cattle drank and drank. We don't know how much water lies between here and Dodge. So we must water the herd where we can.

At Big Sandy Creek, Kansas

Evening

Jeb's back in the saddle. I don't know how well he is. He's limping. Even if he is still feeling poorly, I can't imagine him telling anyone. He'd be too afraid Dovey might hear. Then she'd force him to drink more of her special "anti-venom tea." Imagine choking down milk sweetened with cocklebur juice! Yuck!

There are no trees or hills here to stop the mad, rushing wind. There are no towns, no houses, no railroads, no fences. Kansas is miles and miles of sameness—waving grass crisscrossed by a few dry ditches.

We met an odd little man today. He was traveling across the plain in a wagon. At first, we watched him from a distance. Every once in a while, he stopped, picked up something, and put it in his wagon. When he came closer, we saw that the word "Busted" was painted on the side of his wagon. He was wearing an old Civil War uniform. He approached us.

"Howdy!" shouted Jeb. "Are you a Union soldier?" The Civil War was over thirteen years ago. It was strange to be seeing that old uniform.

"No," he replied, "it's because of them grasshoppers!" The little man then told an incredible but true story. Four years ago this month, he said, a plague of grasshoppers attacked his farm. They crawled along the ground and ate everything green in their path. They devoured his corn and oat crops. They stripped his peach trees of leaves. Then they ate other things. They ate the leather off his horses' harnesses and saddles. They even ate a letter he'd been writing on the kitchen table! They ate the curtains fluttering in his windows and his clothes drying on some bushes. When they left, his place was a disaster. The little farmer was ruined.

His once prospering farm had become a wasteland. He had nothing to wear but a flour sack.

Then, one day, a government agent visited him. He gave him a Civil War uniform to wear. He told them how buffalo bones were bringing a fair price in Wichita and Dodge. The little man painted "Busted" on his wagon, abandoned his farm, and became a wandering bone man, collecting buffalo bones for a living.

Cookie says that the whitest buffalo bones are made into fancy tea cups. The rest, though, just become fertilizer.

Later

My heart is thumping so hard I can hear it in my ears. It's Jeb! He's my thrill! After dinner, I walked over to the buggy to get my diary and pen. I heard someone following me. I turned around. It was Jeb.

"Here," he said, hurriedly placing something in the palm of my hand. It was a small gift wrapped in blue tissue tied with a white ribbon.

"For me?" I asked, timidly. He is so shy, it makes me shy.

He nodded. "Yes," he murmured, "for you."

I gently untied the bow and peeled back the paper. There lay the beautiful mother-of-pearl tucking combs I had admired in Doan's Store!

"Oh, Jeb," I said, letting out a big sigh. I reached out and squeezed his hand. "I didn't know you cared!"

Jeb paused and looked down. With the heel of his boot, he drew half-circles in the dirt. After a short pause, he answered. "Oh, I do care, Miss Hallie. I care a lot."

He was gone before I could even say, "Thank you!"

How will I ever fall asleep with such sweet thoughts in my head?

Friday, July 26, 1878
At Bluff Creek, Kansas

Something funny happened today even though it's probably not nice to laugh. This afternoon, two of our big steers saw a heap of earth rising up out of the prairie. They began bawling and made a run for it. I don't know what they thought they'd find there. Anyway, they began to paw the mounded earth and toss it with their horns. Then a woman came running out from an

131

opening in the ground below. She had her sunbonnet in her hand. She began beating our steers with that hat.

When she saw us, she yelled, "Come and get your blasted steers off my roof!" But it was too late. The roof of her dugout house went ahead and caved in. Both steers landed in the lady's bed!

We camped nearby so we could fix the lady's roof. She lives way out here with her husband, their three children, and a young lady who is the children's teacher. You should see their house. It is built into the side of a canyon and is made of prairie sod. Grass grows on the roof. On the inside, it's very dark, like a cave. But the lady tries hard to make the home cozy and clean. Even though the floor is made of dirt, it's not dusty. That's because she sprinkles it daily with water and salt. To keep the dust down, she plastered newspapers on the dirt walls and flour sacks onto the dirt ceiling.

"It's not much to look at but it's still home," she says. "A soddie don't cost nothin' to build, it don't catch fire, and it keeps the sandy wind out!" The only problem, she admits, besides the bedbugs, fleas, and snakes, is when it rains. Mud and water collect in the flour-sack ceiling and make it sag. How does she solve the problem? She twists table forks into the ceiling to channel the water into dishpans below!

She's nice. She invited Dovey and me to sleep in her children's trundle bed. On the wall above the bed is a coal shovel with a snow scene painted on it. It's hung on a red ribbon. Above the stove hangs a framed, cross-stitching that says Home, Sweet Home. Home, Sweet Home. How I long for home. May I never take it for granted, once I get it back.

Saturday, July 27, 1878
On Bluff Creek, Kansas

Morning

Dovey and I spent a good hour picking fleas off each other this morning. We have little red welts all over our bodies that itch. It was a treat to sleep in a bed last night, but that straw mattress sure is infested with bugs. I don't think I'd like to live in a soddie.

The lady picked some onions, squash, and melons from her garden and gave them to us. She was grateful because we had camped our herd in her field. Cow chips, she said, make great fuel. There are few trees around here.

Tonight, when we make camp, Cookie will chill the melons in the springs of a creek. Then we'll have watermelon slices (sprinkled with salt!) for our bedtime snack. That cold, sweet juice dribbling down my chin will remind me of home, sweet home—

Monday, July 29, 1878
6 miles south of Dodge City, Kansas,
on Mulberry Creek

Evening

We've finally come to the end of the trail. This afternoon, we rode up Seven Mile Hill and, at last, looked down the slope to Dodge City. Now that we've reached the Cowboy Capital of the World, I should be jumping up and down for joy, shouldn't I? After all, isn't that why I originally came on this cattle drive, to get to Dodge? When we left the ranch, I could dream of nothing but the exciting Dodge City with its ritzy hotels and fancy restaurants and big stores. Now that I'm here, why am I so sad?

We can see at least fifty trail herds grazing up and down the valley of the Arkansas River. Jeb rode on into town to meet with Ray. I hope he has lined up a buyer. In this heat, I'd hate to have to trail the herd all the way to Ogallala, Nebraska, to sell it.

Tuesday, July 30, 1878
In Dodge City, Kansas

Afternoon

As Dovey and I drove up to the hotel, I saw Ray, Will, Henry, John R., Jeb, and the rest of our cowboys standing on the sidewalk. As soon as they saw us, they came rushing out to meet us with open arms. I was fairly lifted out of the buggy. My feet never touched the ground while I was carried inside the Dodge House. Every step of the way, the cowboys in loud voices proclaimed me the Queen of the Old Chisholm Trail. I was carried upstairs and deposited in an elegant room. My blues vanished. I was giddy with joy.

After soaking in a warm bubble bath, I had lunch on a tray in my room. I was bone tired. I climbed up into the high feather bed, slipped between the cool, soft cotton sheets and fell into a deep slumber.

Evening

I got all dressed up tonight, hoping to shine for Jeb. I wore my blue silk. I even wore my new hair combs, hoping he would notice. But he didn't even show up for our little celebration. Instead, he stood watch over our herd camped outside of town. Cookie said that Jeb wanted to spend one last night with the cattle. We're loading them into boxcars tomorrow morning. Duty calls Jeb, not adventure. Here he's given up a night on the town to watch over some restless cattle. I doubt there's another man as fine as he is between here and the Río Grande. He may be soft-spoken but he has true character. Hmmm! Now what was it that Fort Worth palmist said?

Anyway, despite his absence, the rest of us had a wonderful dinner and party in a splendid room downstairs in our hotel. The fellows made me feel like the Belle of the Ball. Those fiddlers never took a break. I danced every dance. Will was particularly attentive. He kept cutting in on my dance partners. His face looks so funny. It's white where he shaved off his beard but the rest is sunburned. I think the boys lifted their glasses and made over fifty toasts—to Texas, to Sam Houston, to El Tuerto, but mostly to Mister Ab. They drank a lot of toddies. I don't imagine they'll feel very spry come morning.

Wednesday, July 31, 1878
In Dodge City, Kansas

I rose before daylight to be at the stockyards when Jeb arrived with the herd. Our herd fetched a fair price, thanks to the good spring grass along the trail. Ray said our four-year-olds sold for $25 a head! Won't Papa be pleased!

I waited at the railroad station beside great piles of buffalo bones. They were to be shipped to Kansas City. The skulls of the big bull buffaloes were still decorated with short, thick horns.

Jeb, Ray, and the buyer from St. Louis rode up at the same time. Ray was all clean and slicked up, but Jeb was still grimy and bearded. He looked beat. Even so, he was so handsome. I'm secretly glad he didn't come into town last night. Some girl might have taken a fancy to him.

Jeb got down off his horse. He loosed El Tuerto's bell and shouted, "Squeeze 'em in, old buddy!" El Tuerto and Ole Red headed straight for the railroad corrals. Two thousand Rockin' W's crowded on their heels. Mrs. Bubbies and the little dogies pulled up the rear. Soon they were on a run. The ground was shaking. Inside the gate, El Tuerto and Ole Red jumped aside and rested. The herd swarmed and milled against the far side of the corral. With long metal-tipped poles, cowboys prodded our cattle up the chute and into the cars. The bulls with a horn spread more than seven feet across had trouble getting through the freight car door.

As the train pulled out for Kansas City and then on to St. Louis, El Tuerto, Ole Red, Mrs. Bubbies, the two buffalo calves, and the other gentle cows we were keeping to take back to Texas stretched their necks over the top rail of the corral and watched them go. El Tuerto threw back his head and bawled pitifully. Jeb reached in his saddlebags and took out some shelled corn for him and the others. We would never see those sweet cattle again. It was a terribly sad moment.

Thursday, August 1, 1878
In Dodge City, Kansas

We can't find El Tuerto. Yesterday afternoon, Jeb took him, the other cattle, and the horses we had not sold over to Ham Bell's camp yard. This morning, all the animals were there but El Tuerto. Jeb bought a new bell and put it on Ole Red's neck. He's the lead steer now. After eleven years, why did El Tuerto leave? He has been so mopey since Mister Ab's death.

Our outfit has split up. Everybody's going different directions. The Rowdy King Boys signed on with an outfit heading north for the Platte River. Cookie, Joe, Bud, and Ed are going south. They're taking the horses, cattle, buffaloes, buggy, and wagons back down the trail to the ranch. Dovey was sad to see Cookie go. I have a feeling they might have some news for us once we get back to Texas.

You should have seen how high Ole Red held his head when he led the group down the trail back to Texas. His new brass bell was just a-ringin'! Ray's gone, too. He left for home by train this morning.

Will King was a lot of fun but that's about it. I doubt he will ever settle down. Life with a wife and kids would be too tame for him. He'd always be running off, leaving his wife behind, looking for the next adventure. I pity the poor woman who falls for his cute dimples. He'll make a lousy husband!

Dovey and I bought our tickets when we saw Ray off at the station. Tomorrow morning we'll catch the 6:59 to Galveston. Then we'll board another train to San Antonio where Mama and Papa will be waiting for us. This will be my first train ride. I can't wait.

I've seen very little of Jeb. I wonder what his plans are? The last time I saw him, he was walking down Main Street in brand new clothes. His hair was oiled and he was wearing button shoes! He ducked into a pineboard photographer's studio. He's probably getting his picture taken for a sweetheart back home. I guess those tucking combs didn't mean as much as to him as I thought they did.

Friday, August 2, 1878
At the train station in Dodge City, Kansas

Morning

I waited on the platform until the last possible moment hoping Jeb would appear. But he never came!

I'm choking back the tears. Finally, Dovey and I were forced to load our trunks and board the train. The conductor has already collected our tickets. Any minute now, I'll hear the engineer blow the whistle and we'll pull out of the station. If Jeb's not here by then, I think my heart will break.

To get my mind onto something else, I decided to write in my diary. It helps to center me when I'm troubled. Otherwise, I'd just sit here in the passenger car and stare out the window, searching for Jeb.

I'm a mess of emotion. I'm sad the trail drive is over but I feel the tug of home. I can't wait to see everybody back at the Rockin' W. I'll hitch up a cart to Samson and Delilah and Gussie can ride in it! Mama will have the baby soon. Won't Papa beam with pride when he hears the price we got for his Longhorns! I bet China Doll has already had her kittens! I hope she had at least three so Gussie, Dovey, and I can each have one of our own!

Now I'm feeling better. Oh, before I forget. I wanted to write down this interesting idea I had while at the stockyards on Wednesday. I had a chance to see a lot of different kind of cattle while we waited our turn to load. I noticed that the shorthorns had more meat on their bones than our Longhorns. Lean and scrappy

Longhorns have been the perfect cattle to endure the long drive to Kansas. But that's all changing, Ray says. There will be no more long cattle drives. The railroad's coming to Victoria, he says. Maybe Papa and I could breed a Longhorn with a shorthorn and get a fatter cow. It would bring an even higher price than our Longhorns do! What kind of animal would we get, I wonder, if we crossed a Longhorn with one of the buffalo calves? A cattalo?

For a new breed, I'll need to come up with a new brand and register it at the courthouse. Let's see. What about HL or Rockin' HL or Circle H . . .

JH

Pulling out of the Station

Later

So much has happened since I last wrote on these pages. Do you see that "JH" on my last entry? I didn't write that. Jeb did! He's on this train! I didn't know it at the time, but he was looking over my shoulder as I was writing in this diary. When I came to the part about creating a new cattle brand, he reached over, picked up my pen, and wrote "JH." He says the "J" is for Jeb and the "H" is for Hallie! He wants to register a brand using both our names. Is he thinking what I think he's thinking? Oh, I hope so! Won't Mama be pleased!

Dovey sensed that Jeb wanted a private word with me, so they switched seats. Without saying a word, Jeb handed me a small photograph of himself. He said it was for my locket. I opened my locket and put it in. It fit perfectly. I thanked him and squeezed his hand. Shyly, he then asked if he could have a lock of my hair. I nodded yes. With his pocket knife, he cut a little curl and put it in his left vest pocket. He put it over his heart! Oh! How romantic!

I know he loves me deeply, though I haven't yet heard the words. And I love him, too—until death do us part.

Now I remember what that palmist, Madame Henry, had said about the man she saw in my future. "Still waters run deep," she had said three times. She was describing Jeb, that's for sure. Gentle yet strong, he's the right man for me.

I wonder if they have any chinaberry trees down at Jeb's Circle C Ranch? If they don't, by golly, I'll have to plant us a tall one—right outside our bedroom window.

Life Along the
Chisholm Trail

1878

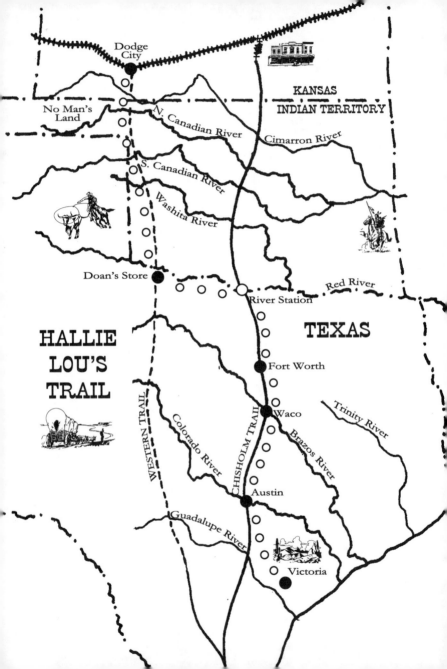

The History of the Chisholm Trail

At the close of the Civil War, Texas was in ruins. Even though there had been little fighting on its soil, Texas was broken by the war. Confederate money was worthless. As weary Texas soldiers plodded homeward, they passed abandoned plantations and farms. Tall weeds grew in what used to be cornfields. Buildings were crumbling, fences falling down, and gates broken off their hinges.

In the brush country of South Texas, ranchers found their corrals empty. While they had been at war, their livestock had been neglected. Their cattle had wandered off in search of juicier grasses, eventually running with the wild herds on the open range. Left untended, these hardy cattle multiplied rapidly.

By war's end, Texas possessed between three and six million Longhorns—most of them wild and unbranded. Cowmen were free to rope, brand, and sell all the Longhorns they wanted. But who would buy them? Nobody within reach wanted to buy any cattle. With so much beef available, Texans were certainly not interested in buying any cattle, even if they did have the money to do so. Locally, a Longhorn was worth only two dollars.

In the cities of the North, on the other hand, a Longhorn sold for forty dollars. Northerners were starved for beef. During the war years, they had almost wiped out what little livestock they had. Generally, they raised their cattle on farms. Their herds were small and kept in fenced pastures. As a result, the growing northern population quickly consumed its wartime supply of beef.

So, in 1865, the Texans had the cattle and the Northerners had the money. The problem was how to link the two groups. In 1866, a few ambitious Texas cowboys mounted large trail drives to the North. They drove more than 260,000 cattle to assorted markets. Some went east to Louisiana where they shipped their herds by boat to meat-packing plants in St. Louis, Missouri. Another trail outfit led by Oliver Loving and his partner, Charles Goodnight, drove a herd westward through dangerous Indian country to New Mexico. They had hoped to sell to Rocky Mountain miners. Most trail drivers, though, followed the safer Shawnee Trail. It led them out of Texas through Indian Territory and on to Missouri. There they loaded their cattle onto train cars bound for Chicago beef-processing plants. Some of these cowboys happily reported selling Longhorns for the unbelievable price of sixty dollars a head!

But not all cowboys had such a pleasant experience driving their cattle to the northern market. Outlaws lurked along the Shawnee Trail, stopping the herds and demanding payment to let them pass. If a trail driver refused these blackmail demands, he was often whipped and robbed and all his cattle stolen.

These cowboys had other nasty run-ins with rifle-toting farmers in Arkansas and Missouri. The farmers hated the Texas cowboys trailing their cattle across their land. Longhorns trampled their wheat and corn crops. Longhorns also carried the tick-borne disease, Texas fever, which did not harm them but did infect domestic cattle. Farmers feared that exposure to the Longhorn cattle would cause outbreaks of Texas fever among their herds. To contain the spread of this disease, many states, including Colorado, Nebraska, Kansas, Missouri, Illinois, and Kentucky, either barred or restricted the trailing of Texas Longhorns across their borders. After encountering so many obstacles, many cowboys who went up the Shawnee in 1866 became discouraged. They resolved never to trail cattle north again.

Cattle trailing might have ended at that point had not Illinois cattle buyer Joseph G. McCoy stepped in. He established a marketplace for cattle away from settled areas but on the Kansas Pacific Railway line in Abilene, Kansas. Abilene was near the center of the mostly uninhabited Great Plains, then a sea of grass. McCoy built stockyards near the railroad line. He managed to persuade Kansas officials not to enforce the quarantine law at Abilene in order to attract Texas herds.

McCoy advertised his new Abilene cattle yard. In 1867, 35,000 head of cattle were trailed to Abilene. Abilene was the main railhead-market for Texas cattle until the quarantine was renewed in 1873. The main cattle path from Texas to Abilene was the Chisholm Trail.

The first herd to take the Chisholm Trail from Texas to Abilene belonged to O.W. Wheeler and his partners. In 1867, they bought 2,400 steers in San Antonio and headed to Abilene. At the North Canadian River in Indian Territory, they saw wagon tracks and followed them. The tracks were made by an Indian trader named Jesse Chisholm. At first, the route Wheeler's cowboys took to Kansas was called the Trail, the Kansas Trail, the Abilene Trail, or McCoy's Trail. Eventually, though, Texas cowboys gave Chisholm's name to the entire trail from the Río Grande to central Kansas.

One historian said that the Chisholm Trail is like a tree. The roots were the feeder trails from all over South Texas. The trunk was the main route from San Antonio across Indian Territory. The branches were extensions to various railheads in Kansas. When Abilene ceased to be a cattle market, the trail might end at Ellsworth, Junction City, Newton, Wichita, or Caldwell, Kansas. When the railroad reached Dodge City, the trail shifted westward. This new route, the Western Trail, was blazed through Texas by way of Fort Griffin and Doan's Store.

Once on the Chisholm, cattle did not follow an exact trail except perhaps at a river crossing. Herds spread out to find grass. The animals grazed along for about ten to twelve miles a day. Lean Longhorns raised in the scrubby mesquite country of South Texas grew fat on nutritious Central and North Texas grasses.

To handle 2,500 cattle, a trail outfit might consist of a trail boss, eight to ten cowboys, a cook, and a horse wrangler. Three months of trailing cost from sixty to seventy-five cents a head. This was immensely cheaper than shipping the herd by rail.

Once the Plains Indians were subdued, ranches popped up all over Texas. Barbed wire fences were erected in the path of the cattle drives, blocking their migration northward. The end truly came, though, when Kansas enacted a quarantine law in 1885. Texas cattlemen then shifted to moving their cattle northward by rail from Texas cities. The last year for the Chisholm Trail was 1884.

The Chisholm Trail was only in operation for seventeen years, from 1867 to 1884. Yet, in its brief existence, it was followed by more than five million cattle and one million mustangs. This was the greatest migration of livestock in the history of the world. The Chisholm Trail provided a steady source of income that enabled the Texas economy to recover from the ravages of the Civil War. The cattle industry was invigorated anew and the state of Texas forever bound to the image of a brash young cowboy astride a bucking bronco.

Women on the Cattle Drives

When we think of cattle drives, we think of men. Our minds conjure up images of cowboys on horseback galloping over dusty prairies. Movies, books, and songs relate the hardships faced by men on the road to Kansas: night stampedes, flooded river crossings, prairie fires, thunderstorms, outlaws, drought, disease, famine, rattlesnakes, and hordes of Indians with bows, arrows, knives, and guns.

To associate men with cattle trailing would be correct. The cattle drive was a distinctly male province. With the men gone up the trail, the women had to stay behind to look after the ranch. Although it is true that a "calico on the trail was as scarce as sunflowers on a Christmas tree," a few women did venture up the trail. Some, fortunately, left a record of their exciting adventures.

In April of 1871, Amanda Burks left her home in Banquete, Texas, and hit the Chisholm Trail with her servant, her husband, ten cowboys, the cooks, and a thousand head of cattle. At first, Amanda personally drove her horse-drawn buggy. She soon discovered

Larry T. Jones III, Collection, Austin

154

this was not necessary. Without her guidance, the two brown ponies easily followed the slow-moving herd. The buggy could pull itself. Once she realized this, Amanda curled up in a comfortable position, fastened the reins, and took a nap.

Mary Taylor Bunton found beauty in nature when, in 1886, she accompanied her husband's outfit up the trail from Sweetwater, Texas, to Coolidge, Kansas. Wildflowers bedecked the "old Chisholm Trail," said Mary. "I was fond of flowers. . . . Sometimes I would fill my buggy and decorate my horses' bridles and harness with the gorgeous blossoms, then I would weave a wreath for my hair and a chaplet of flowers for my shoulders." As Mary rode along, bob-whites called from the tall grass and mockingbirds sang from the trees.

All was not as blissful as it seemed. Beneath many of those trees lurked danger. As many as six or eight

Facing Page: Lizzie Johnson Williams was a tough Texas Cattle Queen and a shrewd businesswoman. In 1871, she registered her own brand. She rounded up abandoned Longhorns, branded them, and put together a good size herd. Several times, she took her herds up the Chisholm Trail to the Kansas market. She grew rich, eventually amassing a quarter of a million dollars.

rattlesnakes could be coiled up at the bottom of a tree, basking in the sun. The countryside crawled with rattlesnakes. Mary had to take care wherever she walked. "I had to watch out every moment," she said. Even as she rode along in her buggy, the rattlers would hiss as they lay alongside the road.

Lizzie Johnson Williams also took to the trail in her buggy. She has been called the "Texas Cattle Queen" because she is one of only two Texas ranch women known to have gone up the trail with her own herd. Lizzie was an accomplished woman. Besides being a cattle rancher, she was also a schoolteacher, a writer, and an accountant.

Lizzie took cattle ranching seriously. She was up before dawn each morning, tally book in hand, counting to see if any of her herd was missing. She kept a time-book of her trail hands' hours. At her home in Austin, she was always fashionably dressed. But, when she trailed cattle with her husband, Hezekiah Williams, she became a no-nonsense dresser. She traded in her city satins, silks, and lace for a simple calico dress, a sunbonnet, and a grey shawl.

That is not to say that Lizzie did not enjoy the finer aspects of life once she was on the trail. The trail hands doted on her, showering her with gifts such as wild fruit, prairie chicken, and antelope's tongue. Each day, they tied a rope around her bedroll to keep off the rattlesnakes. After selling her herd in Kansas, Lizzie and Hezekiah frequently traveled to St. Louis where Lizzie indulged her passion for clothes. There she bought high-buttoned shoes for daytime and slippers with spool heels for evening.

Not only married woman went up the trail. Margaret Borland was a widowed rancher when she trailed to Wichita, Kansas, in the spring of 1873. She bought and sold livestock in Victoria, Texas. She owned a herd of more than 10,000 cattle. She is believed to be the only woman who led a cattle drive from Texas.

When Margaret left for Kansas, she took along her seven-year-old daughter, an even younger granddaughter, two sons, both under fifteen, a group of trail hands, and about 2,500 cattle. She trailed the herd successfully across Indian Territory and into Wichita. Margaret's story, though, does not have a happy ending. Upon arrival in Wichita, she died on July 5 from a fever "superinduced by her long, tedious journey and overtaxation of brain."

Although few women went up the Chisholm Trail with the cattle, the women who stayed behind braved their own share of hardships. They kept the ranch going. Life on the Texas frontier came with no frills; it was tough. As they struggled with the gigantic task of running the home, their children died of yellow fever, Indians burned the stables and stole the horses, bandits poached the cattle, and crops withered from drought.

The diaries of most of these pioneer women reveal that, in order to survive, they had to meet life on its own terms. They did not have the luxury of expecting life to be easy. To complain would not have changed one thing. These pioneer women accepted both grief and joy as their lot. They endured and, in doing so, gave Texas its roots.

Southwest Collection, Texas Tech University

There was hardly a woman on the Texas frontier who could not handle a horse. It was handling her riding skirt that gave her the trouble. In 1878, the fashion was for skirt hems to extend below the feet by as much as a yard. When she was perched sidesaddle, a woman's skirt reached almost to the ground! It would have been scandalous for her to expose an ankle. These super-long skirts snagged on brambles and on saddle horns. It was not until the 1890s that a less cumbersome outfit, the divided skirt, was introduced.

Colorado Historical Society

Ranch women were multitalented. There wasn't a job they couldn't do. In this 1884 photo, the Becker sisters of Alamosa, Colorado, rope and brand calves at a roundup.

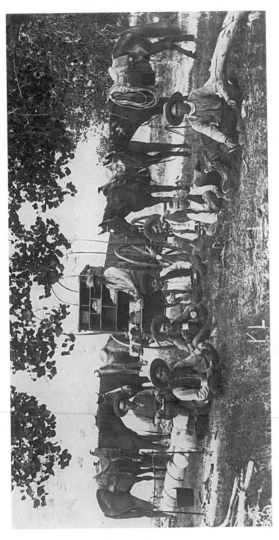

Cattle drives were one long picnic. Cooks were responsible for dishing up three hot meals a day for the trail hands. Once the cattle had calmed down and started to graze, the cowboys had their meals. They filed past the campfire to have their tin plates heaped high with fried meat, corn or sourdough bread, and beans.

9. WHOOPEE TI-YI-YO, GIT ALONG LITTLE DOGIES

Cowboys sang on the trail to keep the cattle from stampeding. The cows were soothed by the sound of the human voice. Cowboy songs were lullabies, meant to put the cattle to sleep. Many of these songs were long and lonesome, timed to a horse's gait as it tiptoed around a sleeping herd. "Whoopee TI, YI, YO, Git Along Little Dogies" was one of the most popular cowboy songs.

162

1.

As I was out walking one morning for pleasure,
I spied a cowpuncher a-ridin' along.
His hat was throwed back and his spurs were a-jinglin',
And as he approached he was singin' this song:

Chorus

Whoopee ti-yi-yo, get along little dogies,
It's your misfortune and none of my own.
Whoopee ti-yi-yo, get along little dogies,
You know that Wyoming will be your new home.

2.

Early in the springtime we wound up the dogies,
Mark 'em, and brand 'em, and bob off their tail;
Round up the horses, load up the chuck wagon,
Then throw the little dogies out on the long trail.

Chorus

3.

Night comes on and we hold 'em on the bed ground.
The same little dogies that rolled on so slow.
We roll up the herd and cut out the stray ones,
Then roll the little dogies like never before.

Chorus

Texas trail outfits passing through Indian Territory often met up with Quanah Parker. He was the son of Comanche Chief Nokoni and Cynthia Ann Parker, a white captive. Besides being a wise leader, he was a shrewd investor, becoming perhaps the richest Native American of his time. He maintained a twenty-two room house near Craterville, Oklahoma, for his numerous children and seven wives, two of whom are pictured here.

Kansas State Historical Society

Travelers on the plains discovered that buffalo chips made great campfire fuel. These "meadow muffins" produced a hot, clean flame, giving off just enough odor to drive away pesky mosquitoes.

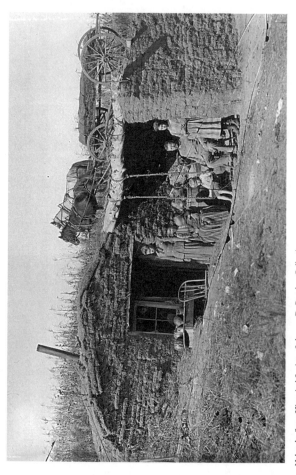

Nebraska State Historical Society, Solomon D. Butcher Collection

Sod houses were not much to look at, but they were well adapted to a prairie environment. They were quickly built, cheap, fireproof, windproof, sunproof, and readily made from available materials. The only problem came when it rained. They leaked.

NOTICE!

TO THIEVES, THUGS, FAKIRS AND BUNKO-STEERERS,

Among Whom Are

J. J. HARLIN, alias "OFF WHEELER," SAW DUST CHARLIE, WM. HEDGES, BILLY THE KID, Billy Mullin, Little Jack, The Cuter, Pock-Marked Kid, and about Twenty Others:

If Found within the Limits of this City after TEN O'CLOCK P. M. this Night, you will be Invited to attend a GRAND NECK-TIE PARTY,

The Expense of which will be borne by 100 Substantial Citizens.

Las Vegas, March 24th, 1881.

Instant justice was a hallmark of the Old West. The noose awaited horse thieves and murderers. Desperadoes were often kidnapped by a mob and strung up on the spot.

The main street of Dodge City, Kansas, shown here in 1878, was a welcome sight to the weary Texas trail drivers. Dodge City was the end of the trail and was known as "the wickedest town in the West."

Montana Historical Society

When the trail drivers reached Kansas, the cattle were sold to a northern buyer. Then the Longhorns were loaded aboard railroad stockcars to be shipped to meat-processing plants in Chicago and St. Louis. Longhorns with seven-foot horn spreads had a hard time getting through the boxcar doors.

Janice Woods Windle Collection

At the end of the trail, William and John Rhodes King put on their best clothes and posed for the photographer.

170

Third Eye Photography

About Lisa Waller Rogers

"You can't grow up in South Texas without riding a few horses," says author Lisa Waller Rogers. Though raised in the city, Ms. Rogers spent many weekends and summers on horseback. "I just love horses!" she says, though horses don't always love her.

Once, when she was fifteen, she went to a birthday party for a friend named Karen. Karen's father had rented horses for the girls to ride on Padre Island. Everything went fine—at first. The girls rode down the beach, laughing, talking, and enjoying the soft ocean spray blowing in their faces.

But the jolly ride soon became a nightmare. All of a sudden, Ms. Rogers's horse stepped in a crab hole, tripped and lost his balance. The jolt took Ms. Rogers by surprise. She accidentally dropped the reins. Without the reins, she had no control of her horse—and that horse knew it. In an instant, he was off and running. It was a good thing Ms. Rogers was a quick thinker or else she would have been thrown to the ground. When her horse bolted, she grabbed his mane.

Now the horse was in charge! He ran as fast as his legs would carry him, far, far away from the stables, his hooves pounding the hard-packed sand. There was no stopping him! He smelled freedom! The reins dangled to the ground, far beyond Ms. Rogers's reach. Her friends watched in horror as the runaway horse and his hostage disappeared into the dunes.

"It was unbelievable!" said Ms. Rogers. "I was so scared. My heart was beating in my ears. That horse was crazy! I wrapped my arms around his sweaty neck and hung on for dear life!"

The horse cut over to the highway and got in with the traffic. A truck of teenage boys pulled up alongside them. "They pointed and laughed at me!" she said. "I felt so angry and so helpless, I just burst into tears."

The horse made a right turn and headed to the Intercoastal Canal. They came to a drawbridge. "The bridge was up to let a barge pass under," she said. "A long line of cars was waiting for the bridge to come back down so they could cross the channel. I guess the horse got confused about what to do next because when he came to the raised drawbridge, he stopped. It was my one chance and I didn't let it pass. I grabbed the reins and turned him back toward the beach."

When she reached the stables, her friends were glad to see her as were her parents—who were waiting. The party had been over for some time. "It's funny," says Ms. Rogers. "the whole time I was gone, I was worried about one thing—how much extra money I was costing Karen's father for being gone so long!"

Lisa Waller Rogers wants her history books to be entertaining as well as accurate. Before she begins writing a new book, she spends months in libraries, gathering information young readers will find interesting. She reads old diaries, letters, newspaper articles, and journals written by real people who lived long ago. She discovers how they talked, what they ate, what books they read, what clothes they wore, and what they did for fun. "Histories should capture the flavor of the times, not just the facts," she is fond of saying.

Ms. Rogers's first history, *A Texas Sampler: Historical Recollections,* was a finalist for the Texas Institute of Letters Best Book for Children/Young People Award. Her second book, *Angel of the Alamo,* received wide acclaim for its beautiful illustrations. *Get Along, Little Dogies: The Chisholm Trail Diary of Hallie Lou Wells* is Book One in the new Lone Star Journals series.